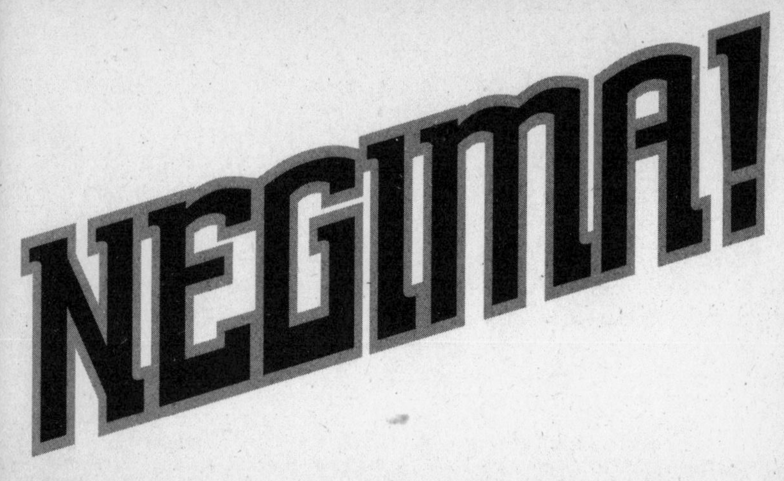

Ken Akamatsu

TRANSLATED BY

Douglas Varenas

ADAPTED BY

Peter David and Kathleen O'Shea David

LETTERED BY

Steve Palmer

BALLANTINE BOOKS • NEW YORK

A Word from the Author

Please excuse my one-month silence. I now bring to you Volume 2 of *Negima!*

You may think that what sets this manga apart is this: "Later, when you read it again from the first frame of the first story, the conduct of the various characters is consistent." But just as you're thinking that, contradictions are already arising in their dialect and expressions. Yikes! There are 31 people so

please overlook that a little. In any case, there are a lot of characters so it's tough remembering them, let alone managing them (ha ha!). However, the class rep, Chisame, and the like are favorites. There is a mountain of various characters and subplots that haven't been introduced yet, so everyone please imagine some various subplots of your own and enjoy! (If you think up any good ones please notify me by mail [ha ha]).

Ken Akamatsu

http://www.ailove.net

Translator—Douglas Varenas
Adaptors—Peter David and Kathleen O'Shea David
Lettering—Steve Palmer
Cover Design—David Stevenson

A Del Rey® Book
Published by The Random House Publishing Group

Published in the United States by Del Rey Books, an imprint of The Random House Publishing Group, a division of Random House, Inc.,New York, and simultaneously in Canada by Random House of Canada Limited, Toronto.
First published in serial form by Shonen Magazine Comics and subsequently published in book form by Kodansha, Ltd., Tokyo in 2003.

www.delreymanga.com

Cataloging-in-Publication Data is available from The Library of Congress.

ISBN 0-345-47120-2

Manufactured in the United States of America

First Edition: August 2004

Honorifics

Throughout the Del Rey Manga books, you will find Japanese honorifics left intact in the translations. For those not familiar with how the Japanese use honorifics, and more important, how they differ from American honorifics, we present this brief overview.

Politeness has always been a critical facet of Japanese culture. Ever since the feudal era, when Japan was a highly stratified society, use of honorifics — which can be defined as polite speech that indicates relationship or status — has played an essential role in the Japanese language. When addressing someone in Japanese, an honorific usually takes the form of a suffix attached to one's name (example: "Asuna-san"), or as a title at the end of one's name or in place of the name itself (example: "Negi-sensei," or simply "Sensei!").

Honorifics can be expressions of respect or endearment. In the context of manga and anime, honorifics give insight into the nature of the relationship between characters. Many translations into English leave out these important honorifics, and therefore distort the "feel" of the original Japanese. Because Japanese honorifics have nuances that English honorifics lack, it is our policy at Del Rey not to translate them. Here, instead, is a guide to some of the honorifics you may encounter in Del Rey Manga.

-san: This is the most common honorific, and is equivalent to Mr., Miss, Ms., Mrs., etc. It is the all-purpose honorific and can be used in any situation where politeness is required.

-sama: This is one level higher than "-san." It is used to confer great respect.

-dono: This comes from the word *tono* which means *lord*. It is an even higher level than *sama*, and confers utmost respect.

-kun: This suffix is used at the end of boy's names to express familiarity or endearment. It is also sometimes used by men among friends, or when addressing someone younger or of a lower station.

-chan: This is used to express endearment, mostly toward girls. It is also used for little boys, pets, and even among lovers. It gives a sense of childish cuteness.

Bozu: This is an informal way to refer to a boy, similar to the English term "kid" or "squirt."

Sempai: This title suggests that the addressee is one's "senior" in a group or organization. It is most often used in a school setting, where underclassmen refer to their upperclassmen as *sempai*. It can also be used in the workplace, such as when a newer employee addresses an employee who has seniority in the company.

Kohai: This is the opposite of *sempai*, and is used toward underclassmen in school or newcomers in the workplace. It connotes that the addressee is of lower station.

Sensei: Literally meaning "one who has come before," this title is used for teachers, doctors, or masters of any profession or art.

-[blank]: Usually forgotten in these lists, but perhaps the most significant difference between Japanese and English. The lack of honorific means that the speaker has permission to address the person in a very intimate way. Usually, only family, spouses, or very close friends have this kind of permission. Known as *yobisute*, it can be gratifying when someone who has earned the intimacy starts to call one by one's name without an honorific. But when that intimacy hasn't been earned, it can also be very insulting.

魔(ま)法(ほう)先(せん)生(せい)
ネギま!
MAGISTER NEGI MAGI
2
赤(あか)松(まつ)健(けん)
Ken
Akamatsu

Contents

NEGIMA!
SEVENTH PERIOD: THE BAKA RANGERS AND THE SECRET LIBRARY ISLAND.
THE BIG GAME PLAN FOR THE FINAL TEST, PART 1

チュン チュン…
CHIRP CHIRP
HUZZAH! FINALLY SOME WARM WEATHER ROLLING IN.
I HEAR YOU, KONOKA-SAN.
WILL YOU TWO SHUT UP AND HUSTLE! WE'RE LATE!
TROMP TROMP
ドドドッ
MORN-ING, NEGI-KUN!
WHAT'S UP NEGI-SENSEI!?
OH! SASAKI-SAN, IZUMI-SAN.
MORNING!
I LOVED DODGE BALL THE OTHER DAY!
WE SHOULD DO IT AGAIN!
SURE THING!

DING DONG GONG
GOOD MORNING, NEGI-SENSEI.
MORNING NEGI.
OH, GOOD MORNING.
MORNING NEGIBOZU.
MORNING!

中等部二年A組
(JUNIOR HIGH SCHOOL DIVISION, SECOND YEAR, GROUP A)
CHATTER CHATTER
OK, WHO CAN TRANSLATE THIS PART?
NEO HORIZON
NO VOLUNTEERS?

SASAKI-SAN! YOU WERE HIGH-ENERGY, GREETING ME THIS MORN-ING. HOW ABOUT YOU?
AH HA HA HA
OH, THANKS LOADS, NEGI-KUN. NO MORE "MORNING!" FROM ME!
NEGI-SENSEI, I'LL TRANSLATE...
HA! CLASS REP'S ALWAYS LOOKING TO SCORE POINTS. IT'S THE HALF-BREED WAY.
HEY! I'M NO "HALF-BREED."
CHATTER CHATTER
. . . . .

(HEAD-MASTER'S ROOM)
学園長室
SO, SHIZU-NA-KUN...IS NEGI-KUN DOING WELL?
QUITE WELL, HEAD-MASTER-SENSEI.
THE STU-DENTS ARE WARMING UP TO HIM, AND HE TEACHES THE LESSONS SO WELL, YOU'D NEVER KNOW HE WAS ONLY TEN.

AS HIS GUIDANCE INSTRUCTOR I HIGHLY RECOM-MEND...
...YOU GIVE HIM A PASSING GRADE FOR THE TIME BEING.

HMM HMM. I SEE. THAT'S FINE, FINE.
AS OF APRIL, WE'LL BE ABLE TO HIRE HIM AS AN OFFICIAL INSTRUC-TOR.
GOOD WORK SHIZUNA-KUN.
PLUMP
WHO TURNED THE LIGHTS OUT?
I'M HERE HEAD-MAS-TER.
OH, GOOD. AH...ONE MORE THING.
THAT WOULD BE...?

I HAVE ONE MORE CHALLENGE FOR HIM. ONE THAT RELATES...
CHURN
...NOT TO HIS TEACHING... BUT HIS WIZARDING POTENTIAL.
CHATTER CHATTER
HUH?
YADDA YADDA
CRUNCH CRUNCH
SIZZLE
BOY. EVERYONE ELSE IS STUDYING LIKE CRAZY.
NO SUR-PRISE THERE!
YEAH. THE HIGH SCHOOL EXAM IS COMING SOON.
SOON? IT'S LIKE NEXT MONDAY.

FINALS. HUNH. I'D BE WORRIED IF I WERE A STUDENT...
...OR EVEN WORSE, A TEACH-
WAIT! I AM A TEACHER! AND YOU'RE STU-DENTS! WHY AREN'T YOU BUCKLING DOWN?
WHIP
UHHH ...
BECAUSE STUDYING TO GET INTO A GOOD SCHOOL ISN'T REALLY OUR CONCERN. WE'RE IN CLASS 2A.

RIGHT. AND SINCE 2A IS ALWAYS THE LAST PLACE CLASS, THE WHOLE THING'S PRETTY MUCH MOOT FOR US.
PAY NO MIND
HEH HEH
HEY HEY THERE
IT'S NOT MOOT FOR ME!

WHAT'S THAT TROPHY OVER THERE THAT LOOKS LIKE A FLOWER?
OH, THAT'S FOR THE CLASS THAT MAKES THE TOP GRADE.
REALLY.

SO, 2A'S THE LAST PLACE CLASS.
MAN, IT'D BE NICE TO WIN THAT TROPHY. BUT THEY SEEM SO DISINTERESTED...
HOW COULD I POSSIBLY MOTIVATE THEM? PROMISE THEM SOMETHING? OR...

SOME SORT OF MAGIC? BUT...THAT WOULD BE CHEATING. THEN AGAIN, CHEATING BEATS LOS-ING...
MUMBLE
NEGI-SENSEI.
WHA!
HUH... OH! SHIZUNA-SENSEI.
THE HEADMASTER WANTED ME TO GIVE THIS TO YOU.
YOU LOOK KIND OF GRIM. NOW I'M WORRIED.

WHAT'S THIS MEAN? "A FINAL CHALLENGE."
PROBATIONARY TEACHER NEGI. FINAL CHALLENGE.
ネギ教育実習生
最終課題
NO ONE SAID ANYTHING TO ME ABOUT "CHALLENGES," FINAL OR OTHERWISE!
I VANQUISHED AN EVIL DRAGON.
I ACQUIRED 200 OFFENSIVE MAGIC SPELLS.
BUT NONE OF IT'LL MATTER IF I DON'T PASS THIS...THIS... WHATEVER-IT-IS.
ドキ ドキ ドキ ドキ ドキ
FLUTTER
FLUTTER
FLIP
ピラッ…
OKAY, NEGI. DON'T PANIC. READ FIRST, THEN PANIC.
THUD
どーーん
ねぎ君へ
DEAR NEGI-KUN,
次の期末試験で、
IF 2A DOESN'T FINISH
二ーAが最下位脱出できたら
IN LAST PLACE, YOU'LL BE MADE
正式な先生にしてあげる。
AN OFFICIAL TEACHER.
麻帆良学園学園長 近衛近右衛門
HEADMASTER, MAHORA ACADEMY
WHAT!?
HAUL THEM OUT OF LAST PLACE BY MONDAY?! IT'S...IT'S...

WHAT'S THIS? WHAT WHAT? WHAT'S GOING ON, NEGI-KUN?
REALLY?
AH HA HA
あははっ
IT'S EASIER THAN I COULD'VE HOPED, ACTUALLY.
BEATS FIGHTING DRAGONS.
IT'S WHAT?
......
ALL RIGHT!
I'LL DO MY BEST.
OH, NEGI-KUN, YOU'RE GONNA BE A REAL TEACHER?!
HEY! WHAT'S THIS?
BACK OFF! IT'S PERSONAL TEACHER STUFF!
OKAY, LADIES, LISTEN UP
TOMORROW'S HOMEROOM IS GONNA BE ONE BIG STUDY SESSION.
THE FINALS ARE JUST AROUND THE CORNER.
AND, UH...IN FACT, IF THIS CLASS CAN'T AVOID GETTING LAST PLACE, WE'LL BE IN A TOUGH SPOT SO...
I'LL BE IN ONE.
EVERYONE LET'S DO OUR BEST AND STUDY HARD.

WHERE DID THIS COME FROM?!

ガヤガヤ

HUBBUB

NEGI-SENSEI, THAT'S A GREAT IDEA.

HEY! I KNOW A STUDY GAME THAT'S ALL ABOUT "GOING FOR IT!"

AND THAT WOULD BE, SAKRAKO-SAN...?

IT'S CALLED 'BASEBALL JANKEN'. SEE, YOU'RE ASKED A QUESTION, AND IF–

おお〜

OOOOHHH

パチパチパチパチ

CLAP CLAP

YEAH! LET'S DO IT!

WAIT A MINUTE! EVERYONE!

HEY!

LADIES, ANY GAME THAT GETS YOU IN THE MOOD FOR STUDYING IS FINE BY ME.

FEEL FREE TO GO FOR IT.

OKAY, THEN! LET'S GO!

いえ〜い

YAY

CHATTER

ワイワイ

ガタッ

BLAM!

WHAT!?

ZAP
OKAY, LET'S SEE WHAT WE'VE GOT.
MAHOR JUNIOR HIGH SCHOOL 2-A. ACCADEMIC YEAR 2002
AVERAGE TEST RANKING (OUT OF 737 SECOND YEAR STUDENTS)
1
2
21
4
BLAH
BLAH
ちょい～
～ん♡
BAKA RANGERS
WE'VE GOT 3 PEOPLE IN THE TOP LEVEL FOR THIS GRADE...
1
100
300
400
500
600
700
737
(RANKING)
(順位)
OH MY...
THE REST ARE IN PRETTY SERIOUS TROUBLE. ESPECIALLY THE FIVE ON THE RIGHT SIDE.
THEY'RE IN SERIOUS TROUBLE, AND THERE'S NOTHING PRETTY ABOUT IT.
GULP.
TAH DAH
WHAT !?
AAAAK!
AW, NOW WHAT ?
STUPID CLASS.
DIFFICULT
PLAY

TO REMEM
〜を思い出す
覚えている
WHAT THE HECK ARE YOU DOING!?
BASEBALL JANKEN. IT'S LIKE STRIP POKER: LOSE CLOTHING FOR EVERY ANSWER YOU MISS.
WELL, THE CHART'S WORST FIVE ARE THE MOST NAKED.
THAT FIGURES
NAUGHTY NAUGHTY
バカレンジャー参上!!
ビシッ
HA YA
IDIOTS AT WORK!
あははっ
AH HA HA HA
コラコラ〜

ASUNA! YOU BLEW ANOTHER QUESTION!
least
ANSWER!
ワイワイ
CHATTER CHATTER
HELLO?! NAKED ALREAY!
アハハ
HA HA
MAN, OH MAN.
WHAT A RAUNCHY BUNCH.

THUD
ど
TH-THIS IS BAD.
REAL BAD.
I'LL BE SENT HOME DISGRACED, AS A TEACHER AND A WIZARD.

SENSEI, YOU GONNA PLAY TOO?
OH, LIKE THAT'LL HAPPEN.

WHAT AM I GONNA DO?
WE'VE ONLY A FEW DAYS TO...

WAIT! YES! OF COURSE! THE GRAY CELL SPELL!
IT'LL TURN THEM INTO GENIUSES FOR 72 HOURS!

DOWNSIDE IS, THEY BECOME DUMB AS ROCKS FOR A MONTH AFTER. IT'S WHY THE SPELL'S FORBIDDEN. BUT IT'S THE ONLY WAY.
RUMBLE
PING
RASTEL MAK-ISTEL.
POOF
HEY! KNOCK OFF THE WEIRD LINGO! YOU'RE CREEPING ME OUT!
A-ASUNA-SAN!
YOU'RE UP TO SOMETHING STUPID, I KNOW IT! GET OVER HERE!
JINGLE

DID YOU EVER THINK, MAGI, THAT SINCE YOU OBVIOUSLY HAVE NO CONFIDENCE IN US TO SUCCEED ON OUR OWN...

...THAT ATTITUDE SHOWS THROUGH, AND WE LOSE CONFIDENCE, TOO?

!!

WHOMP

WITH THE 3
tria fila
BLACK PLEDGE STRINGS
nigra promissiva,
I PLACE A RESTICTION ON MYSELF
mihi limitationem
FOR THREE DAYS!!
per trēs diēs!!
RUMBLE

ASUNA, ASUNA. IT'S TERRIBLE!
WHAT IS IT, KONOKA?
AH, THE BAKA RANGERS HAVE ALL GATHERED RIGHT HERE. IS IT A REPENTENCE MEETING?
ACTUALLY, IT'S A RUMOR BUT...
THE CLASS THAT GETS LAST PLACE ON THE NEXT FINAL EXAM...
WHAT!
THE LAST PLACE CLASS WILL BE BROKEN UP!
B-BUT THAT'S ABSURD.
I DON'T THINK OUR SCHOOL WILL CHANGE ANY CLASSES.
IT SEEMS LIKE YOU GIRLS HAVE BEEN MUZZLED. I DON'T KNOW THE DETAILS BUT MY GRANDFATHER...
THE HEADMASTER SEEMS REALLY ANGRY. HEY, WE'VE ALWAYS BEEN LAST PLACE.
ON TOP OF THAT, THE ESPECIALLY BAD PEOPLE WILL BE SENT BACK A GRADE. WE'LL HAVE TO GO THROUGH ELEMENTARY SCHOOL AGAIN!
HEY!

PUT ON THE BACK PACK ONE MORE TIME...
MORNING!
おはよー♡
HEH HEH HEH
うふふっ♡
AND EVERY-ONE GOES TO SCHOOL IN A GROUP AS FRIENDS.
AH HA HA
あははっ♡
HUUUMMMM
ちょーーん
W-WAIT A MINUTE!
AHAACK!
ズギャーーッ
IT'S A LIE!

NO...BUT IN THE AFTER-NOON NEGI ALSO SAID...
WE'LL BE IN A TOUGH SPOT.
MAYBE, THIS IS THAT "TOUGH SPOT".

THE CLASS NOW IS PRETTY FUN AND IF IT'S BROKEN UP IT WOULD BE AWFUL. ASUNA—
HMMM.
THIS IS BAD. FRANKLY, THE FIVE OF US ARE THE ONES HOLDING THE CLASS BACK.
FROM NOW ON, EVEN IF WE STUDY TO THE DEATH, WE CAN'T MAKE IT BY MONDAY.

OUT OF ALL OF US, I'M BRINGING THE CLASS DOWN THE MOST.
AHOO HOO!

JUST AS I THOUGHT, WITH THIS...
THE ONLY THING TO DO IS LOOK FOR THAT...

GULP, HE SAID THAT THIS AFTERNOON. OF COURSE, WE'LL ASK NEGI FOR HELP.
CANCEL THAT. THE ONE-MONTH SIDE EFFECT OF BECOM-ING FOOLS...
IS 'THAT' WHAT I THINK IT IS?
それってまさか…
ヒエ!
IS THERE SOME WAY TO HELP!?

MA...
MAGIC!!
抹茶コーラ!?
MATTCHA COLA!?
WELL... MAYBE IT'S NOT. MAYBE IT'S JUST SOME SUPER STUDY AID.
EITHER WAY, IT'D BE OUR SECRET WEAPON IF WE COULD JUST GET OUR HANDS ON IT.

YOU'RE BEING RIDICULOUS! THE MAGIC BOOK'S A MYTH!
あははっ
HAH HA HA
OUR CLASS HAS ITS SHARE OF NUTS, BUT MAGIC? NOBODY HERE'S *THAT* FAR GONE.
ASUNA! TELL HER THERE'S NO SUCH THING.
IF I TELL THEM THAT, I'M LYING.
BECAUSE...
I KNOW NEGI'S A WIZARD, WHICH MEANS THIS "MAGIC BOOK" MIGHT BE THE REAL THING.
SPLISH SPLASH

LET'S GO!

TO LIBRARY ISLAND!

BANG

HUH?

MAHORA ACADEMY'S LIBRARY ISLAND

KAEDE= BAKA BLUE
MAKIE=BAKA PINK
ASUNA=BAKA RED
FEI= BAKA YELLOW
YUE=BAKA BLACK
NEGI=+1
HELLO WHAT CAN I DO FOR YOU?
HARUNA/KONOKA/ NODOKA= HELPERS AND UNDERGROUND CONTACTS
2A LIBRARY ISLAND INVESTIGATION BRIGADE (BAKA RANGERS + 1)

NO PROBLEM AT ALL, ASIDE FROM MY BEING POWERLESS.
WHAT!

LIBRARY ISLAND WAS BUILT IN THE MIDDLE OF THE MEIJI PERIOD AT THE SAME TIME THE SCHOOL WAS ESTABLISHED.

IT'S THE LARGEST LIBRARY BUILDING IN THE WORLD WITH MILLIONS OF VOLUMES.

WOW, THIS PLACE IS CREEPY.

I LOVE IT! あいあい♡

YOU'RE A SCAREDY CAT, HUH, MAKIE? こわがりアルねマキエー♡

CREAK

TO TRACK THE MAGIC BOOK DOWN...

...WE HAVE TO GO BACK TO THE CREATION OF MAHORA UNIVERSITY ITSELF.

SSSHHHH

NEGIMA!
OUR MAHORA ACADEMY'S LIBRARY INVESTIGATION DEPARTMENT.
A CLUB THAT INCLUDES JUNIOR HIGH, HIGH SCHOOL, AND COLLEGE STUDENTS.
EIGHTH PERIOD: THE BAKA RANGERS AND THE SECRET LIBRARY ISLAND THE BIG GAME PLAN FOR THE FINAL TEST, PART 2
WHOAH!
WOW! THERE'S TONS OF BOOKS. FANTASTIC!

THERE'S A TON OF BOOBY TRAPS. AND THEY'RE ACTIVE, SO WATCH YOUR STEP.
UPSTAIRS, IT'S PERFECTLY SAFE. DOWNSTAIRS, ANYTHING CAN HAPPEN.
WHAT!
NO WAY!
THAT'S IT WE'RE DEAD?!
SNAP
THIS IS YUE. WE'VE ARRIVED AT BASEMENT FLOOR 3.
STATIC
ROGER!
GOOD LUCK!
ROGER!
STATIC
BY THE WAY...UH... EVERYONE, WHY ARE WE HERE?

WH... WHAAAAT !?
YOU'RE LOOKING FOR SOME SORT OF MAGIC BOOK TO MAKE YOU SMARTER?!
THAT'S KIND OF THE PLAN, YES.
PLEASE HELP US SENSEI.
OH... THAT... BUT...

HOLD ON A SECOND, ASUNA-SAN! FIRST YOU YELL AT ME ABOUT DEPENDING ON MAGIC, AND NOW YOU TURN AROUND AND...
WHISPER
I KNOW, I KNOW.
PLEASE DON'T BUST MY CHOPS, OKAY? THIS IS AN EMERGENCY!
IF WE TANK OUR GRADES, THERES GONNA BE DEEP TROUBLE!

DEEP TROUBLE?
IS SHE TALKING ABOUT WHAT HAPPENS TO ME IF...

OF COURSE! SHE FOUND OUT ABOUT MY CHALLENGE AND WANTS TO HELP ME BECOME A TEACHER, SO I'M NOT IN DEEP TROUBLE!
HOW GREAT OF THE BAKA RANGERS.

HEY, YUE-CHAN. HOW MUCH FARTHER DO WE HAVE TO WALK?
WHISH
WHAT IS IT?!

LIBRARY BRIDGE
秘密の入口
図書館島
LIBRARY ISLAND
SECRET ENTRANCE
図書館橋
ACCORDING TO THE TREASURE MAP I SNUCK OUT FROM THE CLUB-ROOM...
トンッ
TAP
THIS IS WHERE WE ARE NOW.
つい
SLIDE
トントンッ
TAP TAP
FROM HERE WE HEAD DOWN TO BASEMENT LEVEL 11, FOLLOW A PRETTY STRAIGHT UNDERGOUND PATH, AND IT'LL TAKE US RIGHT TO THE BOOK.

IT'S ABOUT FOUR HOURS ROUND TRIP. SINCE IT'S ONLY 7 IN THE EVENING...
...WE CAN MAKE IT THERE AND BE BACK AND IN BED BY ELEVEN. I CAN BE WELL-RESTED ENOUGH FOR CLASS TOMORROW.

YEAH, BUT I'LL BE TOO TIRED TO GO TO MY PART TIME JOB.
WELL, I'LL BLOW IT OFF FOR ONCE. THE MAGIC BOOK'S MORE IMPORTANT.
THIS PLACE IS A LOT CREEPIER THAN I THOUGHT. LET'S GET OUT OF HERE...
CHILL OUT. JUST LET US OLD PROS HANDLE IT...
YEAH, I'M FEEL-ING ADVEN-TUR-OUS.
にょほほ♡
HEH HEH
ME TOO.
HUNH. I WONDER WHAT SORT OF USE-FUL BOOK OF MAGIC COULD BE SITTING IN A JAPANESE LIBRARY?

WELL, THEN, WE'RE OFF.
YEAH!

WHOA! IT'S HUGE. WHAT ARE YOU SUP-POSED TO DO WITH ALL THESE BOOKS?

YOU CAN EVEN GET SOMETHING TO DRINK HERE.

YEP.

WAIT...! WE'RE GONNA WALK ON THE BOOK-SHELVES?

WHAT WERE THEY THINKING WHEN THEY MADE THIS!?

WE WOULD BREAK OUR NECKS IF WE FALL FROM THIS HEIGHT! WHAT DO WE DO?

WE DON'T FALL.

RATTLE

AH!

CRACK

FLAP

AACK!

えーい♡
YOW!
PRETTY COOL, SASAKI-SAN. WHAT OTHER THINGS IS THAT RIBBON GOOD FOR?
IT'S SUPER USEFUL FOR THINGS LIKE GETTING MANDARIN ORANGES FROM KOTATSU. YOU KNOW, THOSE LOW LAP TABLES THAT—
カチン
CLINK
HUH?
GRRR
RUMBLE
ぐらあッ
AAACK!
AAH!
!?
ドカッ
SLAM!
バラバラ
SCATTER
OHHH...A BOOK AVALANCHE
AHH!
NO PROBLEM.
C'MON PEOPLE! WE'RE LOSING TIME! LET'S MOVE!

......
チラ チラ...
GLIMMER
?!
YEAH, THIS IS REALLY GREAT.
HEY YOU! WATCH WHERE YOU'RE WALKING. IT'S DAN-GEROUS.
危ないわね。
UH, RIGHT.
CLASP
HEY! BE CAREFUL HERE TOO.
O-OK.
WHAT'S THIS? YOUR HAND'S ICE. ARE YOU COLD?
KIND OF.

IT'S BECAUSE WE BROUGHT YOU ALONG IN YOUR PAJAMAS.
HERE, WEAR THIS.
UH, THANKS.
......
?
ASUNA IS BEING EXTRA NICE TODAY.
ASUNA! FIRST YOU'RE ALL "I HATE KIDS," BUT THEN YOU TURN AROUND AND ARE ALLL NICE TO NEGI-KUN. WHAT'S UP WITH THAT?
I'M JUST CUT-TING HIM SOME SLACK SINCE HE CAN'T USE MAG...
MAG?
BECAUSE HE CAN'T USE MAGIC.
ASUNA-SAN, THANKS A LOT FOR THE COAT. I'M TOUCHED.
SPARKLE SPARKLE
GET A GRIP, BRAT!
I JUST FEEL BAD FOR HIM, OKAY? HE SHOULDN'T HAVE BEEN DRAGGED INTO THIS IN THE FIRST PLACE.
RINGA DING-DONG
GROUND PATROL SPEAK-ING.
THERE'S A PLACE YOU CAN REST AHEAD. GOOD SPOT TO BREAK AND HAVE LUNCH.
YAY!
I'VE BEEN WAITING FOR THIS.

第178閲覧室
READING ROOM 178
ワイワイ
CHATTER CHATTER
AH, THIS IS TASTY.
WHO WANTS SOME POTATO CHIPS?
OVER HERE!

THIS IS REALLY A MAGNIFICENT LIBRARY.
I KNOW THIS SCHOOL'S STRANGE, BUT WHO'D'VE DREAMT IT WAS THIS STRANGE?
BEFORE THIS, THAT HUGE TREE IN THE BACK HILLS WAS THE STRANGEST THING AROUND. BUT THIS BEATS IT...

THIEVES? DON'T MAKE ME THICK. THERE'S NOTHING GOING ON WITH—

I HEAR HE CLIMBS INTO BED WITH YOU EACH NIGHT.

REALLY!

SHUT UP, KONODA! HE JUST ...SLEEP-WALKS... AND THINKS I'M HIS SISTER, WHO HELPED RAISE HIM...

NEGI-KUN, IS THAT TRUE? DOES ASUNA LOOK LIKE YOUR BIG SISER?

ACTUALLY, MORE LIKE "SMELLS" LIKE HER. IT'S A REALLY GOOD SMELL.

CRAM

ARRGH

HEY!

IS THIS REALLY A LIBRARY!?

THERE'S BOOK-SHELVES.

OH-HHH

I'LL DIE IF I FALL.

AS I THOUGHT: IF WE GET DOWN IN THIS AREA, WE'LL COME UPON A MAGICAL AREA NOT OF THIS WORLD.

WHO'S GONNA READ THE BOOKS WAY UP HERE!?

THIS IS AN INTER-ESTING PLACE.

ゴオオオオ…

DROANNN

RUMBLE

ドドドド…

IT'S CO...COLD. WHY DOES THE LAKE HAVE TO BE COLD?

WHAAH! MY PANTIES ARE SOAKED.

AA-AAH!
WE'RE DEAD. DONE!
スタッ
SKID
PLUNG
ゴォオオオオ..
RUMBLE

ズリズリ..
SQUIGGLE
FINISHED!
KAPUT! AND WORST OF ALL—

MY OUTFIT'S RUINED!
NICE PRIORITIES.
RELAX, MAKIE, WE'RE ALMOST TH— UH OH.

NO, WAIT. IT'S FINE.
WOULD YOU TELL US IF IT WASN'T FINE?

PROBABLY NOT.
QUEEN OF INSCRUTABLE, THAT'S YOU.

ザッ
ザッ
SCRAPE
YOU KNOW, EVEN THE COLLEGE KIDS DON'T GET TO COME HERE.
WE'RE PROBABLY THE FIRST JUNIORS HERE, EVER.

GOTTA GIVE CRED TO THE BAKA RANGERS FOR SHEER GUTS AND ATHLETICISM, IF NOTHING ELSE.
SO— GOOD GOING, GUYS.
C'MON. THE BOOK'S JUST AHEAD.
OH!
ゴゴ..
RUMBLE
ゴトンッ
BANG

IT'S AMAZING! I'VE NEVER SEEN ANYTHING LIKE THIS!
I HAVE. ON MY BROTHER'S PLAYSTATION.
YEAH. IT'S LIKE THE LAST BOSS' ROOM.

LOOK! OVER THERE! THE BOOK IS...
IT...
IT CAN'T BE... NO! IT IS!
WHAT NOW, NEGI?

THAT'S THE LEGENDARY BOOK OF MELUSEDEK!
WOOH
INCREDIBLE! I'VE ONLY EVER SEEN DRAWINGS OF IT! WHAT'S IT DOING UNDERGROUND IN ASIA, OF ALL PLACES?

SO IT'S A LEGIT MAGIC THING?
LEGIT? IT'S THE SUPREME MAGIC BOOK!
FOR THE MELUSEDEK, JACKING UP BRAINPOWER WOULD BE JUST A WARM UP!
NO KIDDING! REALLY!?
NEGI-KUN, HOW DO YOU KNOW THAT'S-?

WHO CARES HOW HE KNOWS!

THIS IS THE ANSWER TO OUR PRAYERS!

WE CAN AVOID LAST PLACE!

WE'LL STAY TOGETHER!

YEEAAAH!

HOLD IT!

NOBODY MOVE! A MAGIC BOOK THAT POTENT IS UNDOUBTEDLY...

...BOOBY TRAPPED!

CLACK

KACHANG

WHOA!

EEEEYAK!

THUD

OUCH!

WHOA!

WHAT HAPPENED?

☆英単語TWISTER☆ Ver 10.5

OW OW OW.

WHOA!

NEGI-KUN, ARE YOU ALL RIGHT?

OUCH!

HUH?

WH, WHAT IS...

ALL WHO SEEK THE KNOWLEDGE HERE...
...ANSWER MY QUESTIONS WITHOUT FEAR.
YEEAAAA!
THWACK
A MOVING STONE STATUE? THAT'S RIDICULOUS!
YIKES!
WHAT THE?!
OH MY...!
THAT IS...
A MOVING STONE STATUE...AND THAT VOICE... SOUNDS SO FAMILIAR... WHERE'VE I HEARD IT BEFORE...
BUCKLE
あわわわ
CLATTERING
ガクガク
GIVE THE JAPANESE EQUIVALENT OF THESE ENGLISH WORDS: <DIFFICULT>
SHOCK
ゴゴゴ...
NO WAY!?
SAY WHAT?
キャーキャー
EVERY-BODY, JUST CHILL!
FOCUS ON ANSWERING THE QUESTION!
HAH
IT'S NOT JUST "TWISTER!" YOU STEP ON OR TOUCH DIFFERENT SECTIONS TO PUT TOGETHER AN ANSWER.

SENSEI, WHAT'S 'DI-DIF-DIFFI-CULT' AGAIN?
WHAT! EASY FOR YOU TO SAY.
IF I TELL YOU IT WON'T COUNT!
IT'S THE OPPOSITE OF 'EASY'! SO, IT'S 'NOT EASY'!!
'MU'
PUNCH
MU
THAT'S RIGHT!
'ZU'
PLOINK
PACHING
'I' RIGHT?
'MUZUI'... WE GOT IT RIGHT.
おお
YEAH!
WE DID IT.
SO, WE GET THE BOOK, RIGHT?
NEXT WORD: <CUT>
HEY!
HO HUM
WAIT A MINUTE!
IF YOU TOUCH THE WRONG PLACE, YOU FAIL.
ASUNA, LOOK! SNIP SNIP.
PINCH PINCH
THAT MUCH I KNOW. 'KIRU' RIGHT?
NEXT WORD: <REMEMBER>
OH, IT'S OK TO USE YOUR FEET.
I KNOW THIS. A-ASUNA MOVE OUTTA MY WAY FOR A SECOND.
'O'
WHINE
THIS IS A PRETTY TIGHT SQUEEZE.
'O'
'MO'...
PANT
NEXT WORD: <BASEBALL>
OH OH OH. 'YA'.
SQUISH
KYU... 'KYU'
UM... 'U'. UHG.
SLAM

WHOOANG!
ドッギャ
OUUUCHH!
WIGGLE
ぴくぴく
YEEOW!
OW, THAT HURTS!
WE'RE DEAD. WE'RE GONNA DIE.
THIS WHOLE TEST IS RIGGED!
TREMBLE
ふるふる
HEY, STONE-HENGE! MOVE IT ALONG, HUH!
BREAKING POINT
ぷるぷる
LAST QUESTION.
RATTLE
ゴゴゴ...
<DISH>
YEAH! LAST ONE!
UH... DISH.
C'MON GIRLS! YOU CAN TAKE WHAT HE SERVES OUT...!
SERVES YOU...? RIGHT! LIKE IN "MAIN DISH."
TWITCH
ぴくぴく
I THINK IT'S... OH! 'OSARA'
GOTCHA!
'RA'
バーン
SMACK
る
RU
'O'
バーン
PLUNK
お
O
'SA'
バーン
BOP
さ
SA

OSARU?
......
'RU'
THAT'S WRONG!
WRONG ANSWER. OO HOO HA HA!
ASUNA-SAN!
MAKIE!
CRASH!
ACK!
SHOOOOOOO
IT WAS ASUNA'S FAULT!
"OSARU" MEANS "FAULT," SO POINTS FOR IRONY!

2A STUDENT PROFILE

STUDENT NUMBER 12
FEI KU

BORN: MARCH 16, 1989
BLOOD TYPE: A
LIKES: APPRENTICESHIP, STRONG MEN, STICKY BUNS
DISLIKES: NEW INVENTIONS IN FOOD AND SWORDS.
AFFILIATIONS: CHINESE WEAPON TECHNOLOGY RESEARCH GROUP.

STUDENT NUMBER 20
KAEDE NAGASE

BORN: NOVEMBER, 11 1988
BLOOD TYPE: O
LIKES: PUDDING, RELAXING
DISLIKES: FROGS
AFFILIATIONS: STROLLING CLUB
NOTE: FROM KOUGA (A COUNTY IN SHIGA PREFECTURE)

HEY, HEY!

H-HELP ME!

FLAP FLAP

NEGI!

CLASP

OH.

ASUNA-SAN.

PLUUMMMMET

NEGIMA!
NINTH PERIOD: THE BAKA RANGERS
AND THE SECRET LIBRARY ISLAND
THE GAME PLAN FOR THE BIG FINAL, PART 3

THIS IS HARUNA, CALLING THE BAKA RANGERS!

COME IN! PLEASE COME IN!

SILENCE

NO ANSWER. THIS CAN'T BE GOOD. ON THE OTHER HAND...

MAYBE THEY STOPPED TO REST AND FELL ASLEEP! UH HUH!

チャプ チャプ..

LAP LAP

WHA--?

HUH...

WHAT?

WHAT IS THIS PLACE?

GGGSSSSSHHH

ドドドド...

OH, THAT'S RIGHT.

WE SCREWED UP THE ENGLISH TEST AND THE STATUE DROPPED US TO WHEREVER THIS PLACE IS.

AW MAN...

THIS JUST GETS BETTER AND BETTER!

THIS PLACE IS BELOW THE LIBRARY?

INCREDIBLE WE SURVIVED, CONSIDERING HOW HIGH A FALL WE HAD

AND WHY'S IT SO BRIGHT? THE WALLS ARE GLOWING!

IT'S UNDERGROUND, BUT DESIGNED TO GIVE YOU A FEELING OF WARMTH, LIGHT AND PEACE.

TREMBLE

ふるふる

IT'S A PERFECT ILLUSION OF PARADISE FOR BOOK LOVERS.

BUT READING ROOMS ARE SMALL, INTIMATE. THIS IS...HUGE.

THE STORY GOES THAT ANYONE WHO'S SEEN THIS ROOM DOESN'T RETURN ALIVE.

HEH HEH HEH

キラーン

フフフ...

えーーっ!?

OH YEAH? IF THEY ALL DIED, WHO LIVED TO TELL THE STORY?

GOOD POINT. LET'S HOPE YOU'RE RIGHT... PRESUMING WE FIND A WAY OUT.

THIS IS CRAZY! WE WANTED A SHORTCUT FOR THE TEST, BUT AT THIS RATE, WE'LL MISS IT ENTIRELY!

CHATTER

ワイ

FORGET THE TEST! WHAT IF WE NEVER GET OUT?

MAYBE THAT STATUE CAN HELP, PROVIDED WE EVER SEE IT AGAIN...

ワイ

CALM DOWN, WILL YA?

WORRYING YOURSELVES SICK WON'T HELP.

OW!

THROB

ズキッ

ASUNA-SAN?!

DON'T STARE I'M FINE. IT'S NOTHING.

YOU HURT YOUR SHOULDER IN THE FALL, DIDN'T YOU. YOU'RE TRYING TO TOUGH IT OUT.

"HEALING MAGIC" ISN'T MY STRENGTH BUT...

RASTEL MASKIL.

STRETCH

WHA...?

D-UH! I'M AN IDIOT!

I FORGOT I DE-MAGICKED MYSELF FOR THREE DAYS. I'VE NO MORE MAGIC THAN MY STUDENTS DO.

I WAS AFRAID OF THIS: NO PLACE TO CLIMB.
THIS IS BAD AND GETTING WORSE.
BOO HOO!
WITH MAGIC, I COULD JUST FLY OUT OF HERE. FLY ALL OF US OUT.
INSTEAD, I'VE GOTTA COUNT ON MY LEADERSHIP ABILITIES.
IT'S MY RESPONSIBILITY AS THE ONE IN CHARGE.
CLENCH
GOTTA GIVE 'EM SOME KIND OF PEP TALK.
BUCK UP, EVERYBODY! WE'LL BE OUT OF HERE, AND BACK HOME, SOON ENOUGH... SOMEHOW!
MEANTIME... LET'S STUDY FOR THE FINAL TEST!
WHAT!?
ST... STUDY!?
HOO HOO!
AH HA HA HA! STUDYING?! AND THE POINT OF THAT WOULD BE...?
TO GET YOU READY FOR THE TEST WHEN WE GET OUT OF HERE.
NEGI-KUN, ISN'T THAT KIND OF OVERLY OPTIMISTIC?

NO... NEGI-KUN'S RIGHT.
I MEAN, GRANTED, ASUNA AND I GOT US INTO THIS SPOT, AND WE LOST THE MAGIC BOOK...
"WHO DID WHAT" ISN'T IMPOR-TANT!
ONLY DOING YOUR BEST ON THE EXAM MATTERS, BOOK OR NO.
Y'KNOW ...IF WE START STUDY-ING NOW...
WE CAN RAISE OUR SCORES AROUND 10 POINTS BY MONDAY'S TEST.
うっ...
GULP
YEAH!
YOU'RE RIGHT!
AT LEAST DOWN HERE, WE'RE NOT HARD UP FOR TEXT-BOOKS.
LOOK! A MATH TEXT OVER HERE!
OKAY! LET'S GET DOWN TO WORK!
ぐぎゅる～っ
GLEAM
BEFORE WE DO...
くす...
CHUCKLE
LET'S FIND SOME FOOD!
おー
YEEAHH
AH! ME TOO! WAIT UP!
シュウウ...
HIIISSSS
HUH...
AH!
パシュウッ
SNNAAP
ONE OF THE SEALS CAME OFF.
THE RISING SUN MAKES IT FALL OFF... SO IT MUST BE SATURDAY MORNING.
WE'VE BEEN HERE A WHOLE DAY. ONLY TWO DAYS LEFT. HOPE WE MAKE IT!

WHA...
WHAT!
COME AGAIN?!
IF 2A FINISHES LAST, NEGI-SENSEI GETS FIRED!!
SAKURAKO, WHY DIDN'T YOU TELL US EARLIER?!
CHATTER
BECAUSE SENSEI SAID TO KEEP IT QUIET.
DID SHE SAY FIRED?
NEGI-BOZU!?
THAT STINKS!
OKAY, PEOPLE! TIME FOR HARD-CORE STUDYING FROM EVERY-ONE, EVEN THE SLACKERS. THAT MEANS YOU, CHISAME.
INCLUDING THE PEOPLE WHO DON'T NORMALLY DO THAT SERIOUSLY.
HEY!
HERE'S NO CHOICE: STUDY OR NEGI'S GONE.
THE PROBLEM IS ASUNA'S BUNCH.
THE FIVE OF THEM CAN'T GET A ZERO ON A TEST IF THEY COMBINED THEIR TOTAL SCORE.
RUMBLE
BIG PROBLEM, PEOPLE!
YIPES
SLAM
NEGI-SENSEI AND THE BAKA RANGERS ARE MISSING!

HUH?!!
どーん
THUD
THIS SOUNDS BAD.

THE NEXT DAY. ONE DAY LEFT UNTIL THE TEST.
OK, WHO KNOWS THE ANSWER...?
I DO! I DO!
RIGHT HERE!
OKAY, SASAKI-SAN.
IT'S 35.
THAT'S RIGHT!
お～～♡
CLAP CLAP
HEH HEH
RIGHT
Y'KNOW, IT'S WEIRD. WE'RE IN THIS REMOTE, UNDERGROUND CAVERN...BUT IT'S GOT EVERY BOOK WE NEED, FULL STOCKED BATHROOM AND KITCHEN...
IT'S TOO GOOD TO BE TRUE.

A BAZILLION BOOKS AND WARM WEATHER. IT DOESN'T GET BETTER.
I COULD STAY HERE MY WHOLE LIFE.
C'MON, YUE! DON'T SLACK OFF!
SNIFF SNIFF
くん くん
MAYBE JUST A SHORT BREAK WOULDN'T HURT...
FEELING AWFULLY GRUNGY. I WONDER IF I COULD...
HEY, MAKIE! WHERE'RE YOU GOING?
I WAS FIGURING I'D...YOU KNOW...
GOT'CHA. SOUNDS GREAT. CARE FOR SOME COMPANY?
I WONDER WHERE ASUNA-SAN WENT? MAYBE SHE'S STUDYING ALONE...
STRANGE. WITH ALL THE WATER, YOU'D THINK THE BOOKS WOULD BE MILDEWED. BUT THEY'RE PRISTINE.
THE BOOKS AREN'T FILED IN ANY ORDER. WHO BUILT THIS SORT OF PLACE!?
AH, THE SECOND SEAL ON MY ARM DIS-APPEARED...
TOMOR-ROW MORNING, I'LL BE MY OLD MAGICAL SELF.
THE WATER'S PRETTY WARM.
YEAH WHEE

WHAT !?
ドドド
ド...
GGSSSSSSHHH
AACK! NEGI-KUN'S A PERVE!
OH NO!
YIKES!
I'M SORRY.
WELL WELL.
むんずっ
JERK
KOOCHIE-KOO! NEGI-KUN, YOUR FACE IS BRIGHT RED. HOW CUTE!
TEACHERS AREN'T CUTE!
HEE HEE
キャッ
キャッ
H-HEY, LET ME GO.
NEGI-BOZU, HOW PRECOCIOUS. ONLY TEN YEARS OLD BUT YOU'RE CHECKING OUT NAKED GIRLS!
じたばたっ
STRUGGLE
GIGGLE
キャイーキャイー
I THOUGHT I NOTICED HIM HANGING AROUND THE BATH HOUSE THE OTHER DAY...
KIDS GROW UP SO FAST THESE DAYS.
キャイ♡
SHRIEK
MAYBE HE'S LOOKING FOR A NURSE-MAID!
ALL RIGHT, THAT'S ENOUGH!
ぷるん♡
PLUMP
UH... THAT...
I...

I'M AN ENGLISH GENTLE-MAN!
AS SUCH I'VE NO INTEREST IN NAKED FEMALE BODIES! NONE AT ALL. ES... ESPECIALLY YOURS!
きっぱり
WHAT ?!
AH!
ガーン
UH OH!
WHOMP!
THAT'S CRUEL, SENSEI.
うわ～ん
HE'S SAYING WE'LL NEVER FIND HUSBANDS BECAUSE OUR BODIES AREN'T INTERESTING!
WHAAAAAA!
NO, I MEANT IT'S INAPPROPRIATE THAT I–
HA HA HA!
THAT'S IT! I'M OUTTA HERE!
ぴゅ～
SKEEDADDLE
OH, NEGI-BOZU!
あ～ん
SHUCKS
LET'S HAVE SOME FUN, NEGI-KUN!
"NO INTEREST IN NAKED FEMALES." THAT'LL CHANGE IN A FEW YEARS.
MAYBE NOT. AFTER ALL, HE'S AN 'ENGLISH GENTLEMAN'.
うひひひ
HEE HEE HEE
ドドド...
GGGSSSSSHHH
ゴポン
LURCH
ブーン
HUUMMMM
HUMPH. CRAZY GIRLS. MY HEART'S POUNDING.
ザッパーン
KERPLUNK
GGGSSSSSHHH
ドドド...
EH?
WHAT KIND OF TEACHER LETS HIMSELF GET INTO SUCH...
WHAT WAS THAT?
ガサッ
RUSTLE
IS THAT YOU, ASUNA-SAN?
WOW.

パァァ…
GLIMMER
……!!
THAT FEELS GOOD.
TRICKLE
AHH.
ホケー
……
WHO'S THERE?
HUH…
HAH
WHAT AM I DOING ?!?
SOME ENGLISH GENTLEMAN. I'M TURNING INTO A PEEPING TOM.
?!

HEY, YOU!
WHAT'D YOU THINK YOU'RE DOING, NEGI-BOZU?
IT... IT WAS AN ACCIDENT!
BANGING YOUR HEAD'S AN ACCIDENT! YOU, YOU PERVERTED RUNT, WERE STARING AT MY--
FLAPP
AT YOUR BANDAGE... ACTUALLY. IT'S, UH ...COMING UNDONE.
OH.
I'LL HELP YOU- CHANGE IT.
UH, NO. THAT'S ALL RIGHT.
I SAID COME HERE! LISTEN TO YOUR TEACHER, ASUNA-SAN.
YOUR WOUND LOOKS NASTY. DOES IT HURT?
THIS? NAH.
A TOMBOY LIKE ME GETS USED TO BEING KNOCKED AROUND.
SSSHHHHH
YEAH, WELL IT'S STILL MY FAULT YOU GOT HURT.
YOU PROTECTED ME IN THE DUNGEON...
FOR THAT MATTER...WELL, I KNOW YOU ORGANIZED THIS "QUEST" SO I WOULDN'T GET FIRED IF YOU GIRLS COME IN LAST PLACE. I SHOULD SAY "THANKS."
....

UM... ASUNA SAN...
NO. IT'S MY FAULT.
YOU SHOULDN'T BE HERE. NONE OF US SHOULD.
I WAS JUST SO UPSET ABOUT OUR CLASS BEING BROKEN UP, AND OUR REPEATING A GRADE, IF WE CAME IN LAST PLACE. AND YOU GOT PULLED INTO THE MIDDLE OF THIS WHOLE TH—
......
WHAT?
WE'D BE HELD BACK IF WE FIN-ISHED LAST—
THE ONLY THING I HEARD WAS THAT I'D BE FIRED!
GGGSSSSSHHHH
......
GGGSSSSSHHHH
......
SO...SO ARE YOU SAYING THE STUFF ABOUT BEING HELD BACK AND...
THAT IT WAS GROUND-LESS RUMORS?
I DUN-NO! MAY-BE!
ARGHHH!
I WAS WRONG! THIS WHOLE POINTLESS ADVENTURE IS YOUR FAULT!
OH, WELL THANKS A LOT!
MY WHOLE LIFE WENT DOWNHILL THE DAY YOU CAME INTO IT!
I WONDER WHO YOU'D BLAME FOR YOUR LIFE IF I WASN'T AROUND!
YIPE YIPE
YOU SHRIMP! YOU LITTLE SQUIRT!
SPUTTER

ズキッ
THROB
HUH?
UHHHH...
OW OW OW...
へな へな...
PLOP
ドサッ...
THWACK
WHOA.
YEOW!
OKAY, THIS IS JUST...
...IT'S WRONG ON SO MANY LEVELS...
GULP.
SORRY ABOUT THAT, NEGI.
I HAD A DIZZY SPELL...
EH?
WHAT'S THE MATTER?
YOU'RE REDDER THAN A BEET.
!!
ARE YOU SICK? DO YOU HAVE A FEVER?
N-NOT YET. ASUNA-SAN, YOUR TOWEL.
NOW YOU'RE BARELY BREATH-ING. SOME-THING'S GOTTA BE WRONG...

LET ME CHECK YOUR EYES.
DON'T MOVE A MUSCLE.
!!
PLOP
カァァァッ..
YAAAACK!
HUH.
SHOCK
SOME-THING AWFUL'S HAPPENED!
PANT PANT
IT CAN'T BE THAT BAD!
TROMP TROMP
DUN
I STAND COR-RECTED.
SOME-BODY HELP ME! ASUNA, NEGI-KUN!
RUMBLE
THAT HUGE THING AGAIN!
ASUNA-SAN! IT'S THE ROCK AND ROLLER AGAIN! HE MUST'VE FALLEN DOWN WITH US!
GAHJOONG

2A STUDENT PROFILE
(TEACHER EDITION)

NEGI SPRINGFIELD

BORN: 1994
BLOOD TYPE: AB
LIKES: OLDER SISTER (GIRLS IN GENERAL), HERBAL TEA, ANTIQUES (WANDS)
DISLIKES: BATHS, SLEEPING ALONE
AFFILIATIONS: A PROBATIONARY INSTRUCTOR AT THE JUNIOR HIGH DEPARTMENT OF MAHORA ACADEMY.
NOTE: MELDIANA SCHOOL OF MAGIC, TOP CLASS FOR THE ACADEMIC YEAR 2002.

EEEEYARRRR!

HO HO HO!

NEGI-KUN! HELP ME!

KABLAM

EEYAH! MAGIC ARROW!

MAGIC ARCHER!

WHOOSH

STARTLE

HO?!

MAGIC TEACHER NEGIMA.
MAGISTER
NEGIMA!
TENTH PERIOD: THE BAKA RANGERS AND THE SECRET LIBRARY ISLAND
THE BIG GAME PLAN FOR THE FINAL TEST, PART 4

しーん
SILENCE

MA...
MAGIC ?!

AW, GREAT, NOW I'VE DONE IT.
AND THERE'S STILL ONE SEAL TO GO!
HAH!
RUMBLE ゴゴゴ
I KNOW ABOUT YOUR PLANS. ABOUT YOUR TEST.
EVEN IF YOU DEPARTED NOW...IT WOULD TAKE YOU THREE DAYS TO RETURN HOME.
HE'S GOT TO BE KID-DING!
TH-THREE DAYS!
WE'LL MISS THE TEST! IT WAS ALL FOR NOTHING!
DON'T GIVE UP, EVERYONE!

MY MAGIC WAND WILL FLY US OUT OF HERE IN NO TIME!
SCRAMBLE
SHUDDUP!
HE DOESN'T KNOW WHAT HE'S SAYING! HE'S GOT A FEVER!
M-MAGIC WAND?
I SAID HE'S DELIRI-OUS! IGNORE HIM!
ANYWAY, WE'RE NOT GIVING UP!
WE'LL BE OUTTA HERE BEFORE TOMOR-ROW'S FINAL TEST!
SO YOU ARE DOING THIS FOR ME!
QUIET, SQUIRT!
RING
NOW LET'S FIND A WAY OUT OF HERE! ADIOS, ROCK BOY!
YOU'RE WASTING YOUR TIME! THERE ARE NO EXITS!
SHE'S RIGHT! LET'S GO HOME!
EVERY-BODY GRAB YOUR STUFF.
...AH!
HEY EVERYONE! LOOK NEAR THE STONE STATUE'S NECK!
HMM ?
IT'S THE MAGIC BOOK!

SHE'S RIGHT! WHEN WE FELL DOWN HERE...
THE MAGIC BOOK AND STATUE FELL DOWN WITH US.
THRUST
LET'S GET THAT BOOK!
MAKIE-SAN, FEI KU-SAN, KAEDE-SAN!
OK BAKA LEADER!
YOU THINK YOU'RE POWERFUL, BOULDER BOY?
THAT'S ZIP NEXT TO THE KARATE POWER OF THE PRESIDENT OF THE CHINESE WEAPON TECHNOLOGY RESEARCH GROUP!
YAAAAHHHHH!!
WHAT ...!?
AHOH
AACK!
YAH!
THWAP!
UNFFF!
GOT'CHA!

SWISH
SNAP
HAH!?
YAH!
WHOOSH
YEAH! WE GOT THE MAGIC BOOK!
IT'S THE MIGHTY MORPHIN' BAKA RANGERS!
CLOMP CLOMP
S-STOP!
WAY TO GO!
IF I HAD MY POWER, I COULD ZAP US OUT OF HERE IN NO TIME.
OHHHH...
YEAH, BUT I THINK SHOCK ROCK WANTS IT BACK. HERE HE COMES! WE NEED A SHORTCUT TO THE SURFACE!
BETTER LEG IT ON MY OWN AND HOPE IT'S ENOUGH!
I'D WIN, BUT STILL LOSE
BUT IF I DID THAT, THEN MY SECRET'S OUT, I'D HAVE TO RETURN HOME, AND I'M NOT A TEACHER ANYMORE.
GET DRESSED BUT DON'T SLOW DOWN!
THIS BOOK WEIGHS A TON!
THANKS.
I'VE GOT OUR CLOTHES!
COMBINE BRAIN-WORK AND TEAM-WORK, AND PRESTO! THE BOOK'S OURS!

I ALREADY TOLD YOU: THERE'S NO EXIT.
CLOMP TROMP
STOP RUNNING. SAVE YOURSELVES THE EFFORT.
YOU STOP RUNNING FIRST!

HEY! THERE'S SOME SORT OF DOOR BEHIND THIS WATERFALL!
SOME KIND OF EMERGENCY EXIT!
GGGGSSSSHHHH
HUH!?

KA CHING
WAIT! WAIT!
I KNOW THIS!
REALLY ?!
SPLASH
THE ANSWER'S "READ"!
CLANK
YOU BETTER BE—
DING DONG
RUMBLE
IT OPENED!
GIVE ME THAT!
TROMP TROMP
I NEVER DOUBTED YOU! LET'S GO!
HEY, DID YOU GET THE ANSWER FROM THAT BOOK!?
JUST HOLDING IT MAKES YOU SMART.
WHAT THE HECK IS THAT!?
A SPIRAL STAIRCASE!?
WE GOTTA CLIMB THAT!?
RUMBLE

PANT PANT WHEEZE WHEEZE

THIS IS HARDER THAN CLUB PRACTICE.

SLAM

YIKES!

NAH-NAH! BITE ME, STONE BOY!

HEY! THERE'S ANOTHER PROBLEM ENGRAVED ON THE WALL.

AW, SWELL. A MATH PROBLEM.

'MATH PROBLEM. QUESTION 2. IN THE GRAPH BELOW, DETERMINE THE VALUE OF X'.

問2.数学問題

SHAKE

HE'S CATCHING UP! AND HE DOESN'T LOOK HAPPY!

CRUNCH

GASP

I'LL— I'LL DO THIS ONE.

HMMM. I THINK IT'S... 46 DEGREES.
RATTLE
IT OPENED! NICE GOING, KAEDE!
BUT THERE'S LOTS MORE DOORS!
ARE THE BAKA RANGERS UP FOR THE CHALLENGE?
GASP WHEEZ
'QUESTION 9. WHAT IS THE ENGLISH PHRASE FOR "SAGASU"?'
AH, I GOT IT! "LOOK FOR".
GOOD ONE.
SMASH
'QUESTION 10. WHO WAS THE FATHER OF FUJI-WARA-SHI, A MAJOR FIGURE DURING THE TAIKA REFORMATION?'
OH! I REMEMBER IT WAS A WEIRD NAME! UHM... 'KAMATARI NAKATOMI-NO'.
CRASH
HURRY!
STOP!
SCRAPE
ALL YOU BAKA RANGERS ARE DOING GREAT!
EVEN ASUNA AND MAKIE KNOW THEIR FACTS! THIS MAGIC BOOK'S THE REAL DEAL!
THAT'S RIGHT! WE BAD!
SLIP
AAH!
YUE-CHAN!!

OUCH OUCH
いたた
BLASTED TREE ROOTS...! ARGHH! I SPRAINED MY LEG.
WHAAAAT!? ARE YOU OK?!

LEAVE ME, NEGI-SENSEI. TAKE THE BOOK! AVOID LAST PLACE!
UH UH! NO CHILD GETS LEFT BEHIND.

GET ON MY BACK! I'LL CARRY YOU THE REST OF THE—
UH...
AH...
STAGGER
よろっ...
WOBBLE
ふら ふら

ぺちゃっ
PLOP
"OF THE WAY?" HEH.

SCOOP
ひょいっ
HUH...
THANKS KAEDE-SAN.
CHECK ME OUT. I'M "SESSHA," THE SAMURAI WHO ASSISTS HARD LUCK WOMEN.
THAT'S IT! ONE FOR ALL AND ALL FOR ONE!

ARE YOU ALL RIGHT!?
GASP
Y-YEAH.
WE'VE BEEN CLIMBING FOR AN HOUR! MAYBE TWO! I'M BEAT!
'QUESTION 29. UNSCRAMBLE THE EXPRESSION AND COMPLETE THE FOLLOWING ENGLISH SENTENCE.' "THIS IS A PICTURE: (A) ON SEPTEMBER 21 (B) TOOK (C) WE."
THEY'RE GETTING MORE AND MORE ANNOYING.
THE ANSWER'S C-B-A!
RUMBLE
ドゴゴ
GIVE IT BACK!

CL... CLOSE TO THE SUR-FACE!?
PANT PANT
HEY! LOOK EVERY-ONE!

WHAT...

MY CELL PHONE HAS RECEP-TION!
WE'RE CLOSE TO THE SUR-FACE! EVERYONE HOLD ON WHILE I CALL FOR HELP!

AN ELEVATOR THAT GOES RIGHT TO THE TOP!
B30
1F 直通
作業用
WE CAN USE IT TO GET BACK!
THUD

HURRY EVERY-BODY! GET IN! GET IN!
AAAH! QUICK! QUICK!
TROMP TROMP

YEAH! WE'RE IN!
ALL RIGHT! NEXT STOP: SAFETY!

DING

OVER CAPACITY.

WE'RE OVER-LOADED!

BUZZZ

EEEH...!

NOOOOOO!

BUZZ

TWO DAYS OF OVEREATING AND DRINKING AT THE UNDERGROUND READING ROOM! WE SHOULD'VE KNOWN!

MAKIE-CHAN, I SAW YOU PIGGING OUT THE MOST!

LIKE HELL! I LOST WEIGHT! NOW ASUNA AND NAGASE-SAN, THEY WERE EATING EVERYTHING IN SIGHT...

I CAN'T BELIEVE I'M SAYING THIS, BUT... EVERYBODY STRIP!

THE CLOTHES ARE EXCESS WEIGHT! I SAY WE LOSE 'EM!

SHE'S RIGHT!

YEAH. HURRY UP!

WHO CARES?! WE'RE TOO HEAVY FOR THIS LAME ELEVATOR! DEAL!

OKAY, BUT... I'M ON RECORD AS ONLY STUDYING...

YAH!

FLING

HOW'S THIS!?

BOY, ANY EXCUSE...

BUZZZ
ANYONE GOT SCISSORS?
WE COULD CUT OUR HAIR...
IT'S NOT WORKING.
AAAACK!
CRASH
GRRRAA
HUH HA HA. CLOSE, GIRLS. YOU CAME VERY CLOSE...
NEGI?!
WHOOSH
EVERYBODY GO AHEAD! GO TAKE THE FINAL TOMORROW!
I'M GETTING OFF!

I WILL PROTECT MY STUDENTS!!
EVEN WITHOUT MAGIC, I'M STILL A TEACHER!! I HAVE TO DO THIS!
B30
SSSSHHHHAAA
WHAT?!
DON'T BE CRAZY—!
MONSTER!
I AM YOUR OPPONENT!
NEGI-KUUUN!
NEGI-BOZU!!
HO HA. YOU'RE A BRAVE LITTLE FOOL!
YEAH? AND YOU'RE—
RUMBLE
GRASP
AAH!?
YOINK

KA CHUN
HUH !?
A- ASUNA-SAN!
SWIPE
WHOOSH
WHAT POINT IS THERE IN OUR DOING WELL...
...AND YOUR BECOMING A TEACHER IF YOU'RE NOT THERE TO BECOME ONE?!
YOU'RE TRYING TO ACT LIKE AN ADULT MALE. CONGRATULATIONS: YOU'VE BECOME AS DUMB AS A TYPICAL ONE.
BUT THAT STONE STATUE'S GONNA...
IT'S NOT GONNA DO ANYTHING.
STOP!
DON'T!
SNATCH
WHA--?
YOU HEARD HIM, ASUNA!
DON'T STOP! JUST DO IT!

NOT THAT!
WHOOSH
AAAAHHHHH!
FLAP
FLING
THE M-MAGIC BOOK IS...!?
HUH!?
OH...
PLOINK
CLICK
SMACK! CRASH!
OH...
AAAAH!
BING
CAPACITY OVER OK ♥
YES! WE'RE MOVING.
RISE
WE'RE OUTTA HERE!
WHOOOM

10
HUMMM
15
20
25
WHEW!
THAT WAS CLOSE.
BUT, BUT THE BOOK IS...
AFTER ALL THAT...
"ALL THAT" TOOK US TO MONDAY EVENING.
SO LIBRARY ISLAND WAS A TOTAL WASTE!
HA HA HA.
BUT IT WAS FUN!
1F
CHING
KA-CHUN
WHOA!
THAT'S BRIGHT.
JUNG
WELL, HERE WE ARE.
WE'RE OUT!
UHM... MIGHT'VE BEEN NICE TO KEEP OUR CLOTHES WITH US...
YAY!
15 MINUTES UNTIL THE START OF THE FINAL TEST. WHAT WILL THE BAKA RANGERS DO?!

キーンコーン
DING DONG GONG
THE DAY OF THE FINAL TEST.
中等部二年A組
カーンコーン
(JUNIOR HIGH SCHOOL DIVISION. SECOND YEAR, GROUP A)

THE BELL'S ALREADY RUNG!
AND THE FIVE OF THEM AREN'T HERE YET!
THEY WON'T GET A LOW GRADE. THEY'LL GET NO GRADE!
AHEM... LADIES! THE TEST HAS STARTED. TAKE YOUR SEATS NOW!

THE BAKA RANGERS ARE HERE!!
GASP, GASP WE'RE LATE!
THE LIBRARY GROUP AND NEGI-SENSEI ARE WITH US!
NEGIMA!
ELEVENTH PERIOD: THE BAKA RANGERS AND THE SECRET LIBRARY ISLAND
THE BIG GAME PLAN FOR THE FINAL TEST, PART 5

TROMP TROMP
CUT US A BREAK! WE'RE LATE 'CAUSE WE STUDIED ALL NIGHT!
GASP GASP
NODOKA WAS SUP-POSED TO WAKE US UP AT 1 O'CLOCK!
SORRY!
WE OVER-SLEPT!
WHEEZ WHEEZ
ASUNA! QUICK! WE'VE STARTED.
HEY! TAKE YOUR SEAT.
GASP, WHEEZ... MUH...MY APOLOGIES!
I'M SORRY WE'RE LATE. THIS GIRL INJURED HER LEG.
THE BAKAS. SHOULD-'VE KNOWN.
WHEEZE GASP
GASP WHEEZ
YOU LATE-COMERS WILL TAKE THE TEST IN ANOTHER ROOM.
OH, OK. SORRY.
PLEASE DON'T WOBBLE.
WOBBLE WOBBLE
UH... EXCUSE ME...

LEAVE IT TO US!
WE'LL GET BY WITHOUT THE BOOK.
THANKS FOR STICKING WITH US FOR THE MARATHON STUDY SESSION, NEGI-SENSEI.
WE'LL TAKE IT FROM HERE.
HA HA HA!
WHISK
THEY SEEM ALMOST FEARLESS. AMAZING.
EVERY-THING'S FINE, NEGI.
CLASP
CONFIDENCE IS HALF THE BATTLE. BESIDES...
I THREW THE BOOK AWAY, NOT YOU. SO DON'T BEAT YOURSELF UP. THAT'S MY JOB.
HEH. SERIOUSLY. WE'LL DO GREAT. RELAX.

UH, OK. BUT...
EVERY-ONE, LET'S GO!
YEAAH!
POOPED
ASUNA-SAN, EVERY-BODY... BEST OF LUCK.
I HOPE THEY'RE ALL RIGHT...

ALL RIGHT. YOU'LL HAVE FIFTY MINUTES.

BEGIN.

RUSTLE

TACK TACK

TACK TACK

BOY... THIS IS AS TOUGH AS I THOUGHT. TOUGHER, EVEN.

SWAY

CAN BARELY KEEP MY EYES OPEN...

LOOKS LIKE THAT ALL-NIGHTER WAS A MISTAKE.

HEY! NO TALKING.

特別教室

(SPECIAL CLASSROOM.)

I CALL ON YOU, FRAGRANCE OF FLOWER. FILL MY FRIENDS WITH PURE ENERGY POWER

REFECTIO

SO? DO YOU THINK YOU PASSED?
. . . . . .
WE DID ALL WE COULD.
SLUMP
NEXT TIME, DON'T BE LATE.
AH. THE TEST SHEETS FROM THE LATE-COMERS.
HMMM
HEAD-MASTER! YOU'RE INJURED! HOW--?

OH, IT'S NOTHING. JUST TOOK A LITTLE SPILL.
BY THE WAY, I WANT TO GRADE THE EIGHT LATE-COMERS... PERSONALLY.

WHISK
WHISK

AH, HMMM.
INDEED.

THE ANNOUNCE-MENT DAY OF CLASS GRADES.
HULLABALOO

CHATTER
ワイワイ
CHATTER
ワイワイ
(INFORMATION DEPARTMENT.)
食券コーナー→
FINAL TEST, RANKING ANNOUNCEMENT
ガヤ
ガヤ
ARGH! I'M SO NERVOUS.
OUR SCHOOL MAKES A BIG DEAL OUT OF ANYTHING. I HEAR PEOPLE ARE PLACING BETS.
I STILL HAVE 10 LUNCH TICKETS.
AT LEAST THAT WHOLE STARTING OVER FROM ELEMENTARY SCHOOL IF WE BLEW THE EXAM WAS JUST A RUMOR.
I'M FEELING PRETTY GOOD ABOUT THIS WHOLE THING, ACTUALLY.
MUST BE NICE NOT TO CARE ABOUT OTHERS, YUE!
HURLY BURLY
ガヤ
ガヤ
ガヤ
HEY! I'M AS WORRIED ABOUT NEGI-BOZU AS ANYBODY—!
GULP.
YOU'RE FINE NEGI-KUN. WE ALL DID OUR BEST.
I FEEL CONFIDENT.
UH, YEAH. THANKS, KONOKA-SAN.

SECOND YEAR. GRADE RANKING ANNOUNCEMENT.
THE AVERAGE SCORE FOR SECOND YEAR STUDENTS THIS YEAR IS 73.4. AND NOW,
THE RANKING OF THE CLASS GRADES FOR THE NUMBER 2 CLASS.

FIRST PLACE, SECON YEAR...
PITTER PATTER
WHAT!?
COULD WE POS-SIBLY BE...?

GROUP 2-F. AVERAGE SCORE 80.8 POINTS.
GROUP 2-F! AN AVERAGE SCORE OF 80.8 POINTS.
CLAP CLAP
OHHHH
WITHER
OH NO!

NO SURPRISE 2-A WASN'T FIRST PLACE. BET 50 LUNCH TICKETS.
CHATTER
I TOLD YOU IT WAS IMPOS-SIBLE.

SECOND PLACE, SECOND YEAR...
YEAH! COME ON!
GROUP 2-S. 79.8 POINTS!!
WITHER
OH NO!

10TH PLACE, 2-M.
WE GOTTA BE 10TH PLACE RIGHT!?
UM, THIS MIGHT BE BAD.
11TH PLACE. 2-C.
WE COULD'VE HAD IT, THOUGH...

WAIT, WAIT A SECOND! OUR CLASS, 2-A HASN'T COME UP AT ALL. EVEN THOUGH WE DID OUR BEST.
がんばったのに——
HEY HEY, RELAX. THERE'S STILL 3 CLASSES TO GO.

THIRD FROM THE BOTTOM IN 22ND PLACE...

GROUP 2-P. AVERAGE SCORE 70.8 POINTS.

2-P WITH 70.8 POINTS.

YIKES!

THIS... THIS IS BAD! IF WE'RE NOT NEXT, THEN WE'RE LAST.

PITTER PATTER

NEGI-KUN...

NEGI ...

MAYBE I SHOULDN'T HAVE TOSSED AWAY THAT BOOK...

BUT WHAT ELSE COULD I HAVE DONE?

NEXT IS SECOND FROM THE BOTTOM ...

2-A!!

COME ON 2-A!

THIS IS THE BOOBY PRIZE.

UHMM... GOES TO...

THUMP THUMP

GROUP 2-K. AVERAGE SCORE 69.5 POINTS.
2-K. AN AVERAGE SCORE OF 69.5. NEXT TIME TRY HARDER.
UH..
THAT MEANS...
SIGH
GHAST
CHATTER
CREAK
...LAST PLACE...
...IS ALL OURS?!
SHOCK
OH DEAR. THE STUDENTS TOOK IT UPON THEMSELVES TO START THE ANNOUNCEMENT MEETING.
DASH
UH? WHAT WAS THAT?

SISTER.

I'M COMING HOME NOW.

MY DREAM OF BECOMING A GREAT WIZARD IS OVER.

BUT EVERYONE TRIED THEIR HARDEST...

I'M HAPPY ABOUT THAT.

NO, THAT'S NOT TRUE. NONE OF YOU WERE AT FAULT.
NEGI...
IF I WAS ANY KIND OF A TEACHER, YOU WOULDN'T HAVE NEEDED SOME MAGIC BOOK TO PASS. I JUST WASN'T READY, THAT'S ALL.
TELL ALL TH OTHERS I SAID THANK ...BUT ESPE CIALLY TO YOU FIVE BAKA RANGERS.
THE BRIEF TIME I HAD HERE WAS GREAT.
WAIT A MINUTE! YOU'RE GONNA GIVE UP THAT EASILY!?
MAGI... SOMETHING WILL WORK OUT.
GOOD BYE!
DASH
HOLD IT!
NO YOU DON'
WHOOSH
EEYAH!
YOU IDIOT!
STAY PUT, FOR CRYING OUT LOUD!

LOOK, YOU BUGGED ME BECAUSE I FIGURED YOU WERE, LIKE, THIS BRATTY LOSER ALWAYS DOING STUPID STUFF..
BUT YOU TRIED SO HARD, FOR US, THE GROUP EVERYONE ELSE SEES AS LOSERS. IT WAS PRETTY IMPRESSIVE, OKAY?
A...
ASUNA ...
NEGI-BOZU!
WAIT UP NEGI-KUN!
TROMP TROMP
NEGI-BOZU!
WHAT ARE YOU GUYS--?!?
!!
I CAN'T STAND HAVING YOU ALL PITY ME!
DASH
BYE, ASUNA!
AH! NEGI!
HEY!
ZIP
LOOK OUT!
THWOMP
RATTLE
ACK! SORRY, NEGI-KUN!
SNAP

NEGI-SENSEI!
NEGI BOZU!
THAT'S CRUEL, NEGI-KUN! SNEAKING AWAY WITHOUT TELLING ANYONE!
CHATTER
NEGI-KUN, WE'LL BEG THE HEAD-MASTER ON YOUR BEHALF!
UH...
THAT'S RIGHT. THAT'S TOO HARSH! YOU'RE ONLY A KID.
LET'S ASK TO TAKE THE TEST AGAIN!
NO... I'M SATISFIED WITH HOW THE FINAL CHALLENGE WENT.
HO HUMM. YOU CALLED?
KA
SSSHH
WHAT?!
HEH...
HMMM
HEAD-MASTER-SENSEI!?
MY APOLOGIES, NEGI-KUN...
YOU SEE...
THE FINAL NUMBERS WERE TALLIED AND ANNOUNCED PREMATURELY...
...WITHOUT THE EIGHT STUDENTS I GRADED. THE NEWS CLUB STUDENTS HAVE BEEN DISCIPLINED SEVERELY.
UH HUH
HO HMMM

WHA...
WHAT DOES THAT MEAN!?
DIDN'T YOU HEAR HIM? IT MEANS OUR POINT GRADES WEREN'T ADDED IN!
M- MAYBE—
MAYBE 2-A ISN'T IN LAST PLACE!
SO EVERY-THING HINGES ON US BAKA RANGERS? WE'RE DEAD.
SINCE YOU SEEM SO EAGER TO KNOW...
FIRST OFF, MAKIE SASAKI WITH A SCORE OF 66. WELL DONE.
COME ON! NO WAY! 66 POINTS?
CARING ABOUT YOUR CLUB ACTIVITIES IS FINE, BUT ACADEMICS ARE IMPORTANT, TOO.
YAY
CLAP CLAP
UH, YEAH...
NEXT IS FEI KU WITH 67 POINTS AND KAEDE NAGASE WITH 63 POINTS.
CLEARLY YOU TRIED VERY HARD.
RE-REALLY?
HMPH.
CLAP CLAP
YEAH!
NEXT, YUE AYASE, SHOWING FAR MORE DILIGENCE THAN NORMAL: 63 POINTS.
I'M VERY PROUD, GRAND-DAUGH-TER.
NOT GOOD.
OOOOO
CLAP CLAP
HARUNA SAOTOME, 81 POINTS.
NODOKA MIYAZAKI 95 POINTS.
KONOKA 91 POINTS.
NO PROBLEM THERE.
HEAR HEAR!
CHATTER
OOOH

THUMP THUMP
FINALLY, ASUNA KAGURAZAKA...
71 POINTS!
HUH... ?
WELL DONE, ASUNA-SAN!
TH-THAT'S GREAT!
OOOOOO
OH...
SO HOW DID WE FINISH...?
HAVING RETOTALED THE GRADES...
DUE TO THE HEADMASTER'S MISTAKE THE SCORES ARE BEING RECOUNTED.
THE AVERAGE SCORE BECOMES 81 POINTS. WITH A DIFFERENCE OF .2...
WHAT!
2-A IS TOPS!
I'M A LUNCH TICKET MILLIONAIRE.
10,000 BETTING POOL TICKETS.
WE...
YEAAAAH!
WE DID IT!

HUH... NO WAY... BUT THAT...
SLAP
WE DIDN'T HAVE THE MAGIC BOOK SO HOW IN THE WORLD DID WE...?!
YOU MEAN THIS!?
WHISH
AH!
IF ALL IT TOOK TO BECOME SMART WAS THIS, WHAT JOY WOULD THERE BE IN LEARNING?
CHATTER
YOU SUCCEEDED BECAUSE OF YOUR ABILITIES.
HEADMASTER-SENSEI HAS THE MAGIC BOOK. COULD THAT MEAN THAT...
THAT HE WAS BEHIND THE MAGIC BOOK, STATUE, AND LIBRARY ISLAND... ALL OF IT?!
THE FINAL CHALLENGE WAS DESIGNED TO SEE IF YOU, NEGI-KUN, SHOULD STAY ON AS A FULL TEACHER.
YOU DID SUPERBLY ON LIBRARY ISLAND, DESPITE THE MANY TRAPS.
ALTHOUGH VEN I DIDN'T EXPECT 2-A TO FINISH FIRST! MY OMPLIMENTS O YOU AND ALL YOUR STUDENTS.
YES, YOUR STUDENTS, NEGI-KUN.
FROM THIS POINT ON, YOU'RE A TEACHER AS WELL.
I PASSED?!
OH... THANK YOU!

ASUNA-SAN... I...
HO HMMM
AH HA HA
HA HA HA! GREAT NEWS, HUH, NEGI!
SO...
I'LL SEE YOU AGAIN STARTING THE NEW TERM.
RUFFLE
UH, YEAH. I'M LOOKING FORWARD TO IT.
UN-BELIEV-ABLE!
THAT'S GREAT, NEGI-KUN!
YEAH!
AH HA HA HA
YEEAH! HEY! WAIT A MINUTE YOU GUYS!
LET'S TOSS HIM IN THE AIR!
AAH!

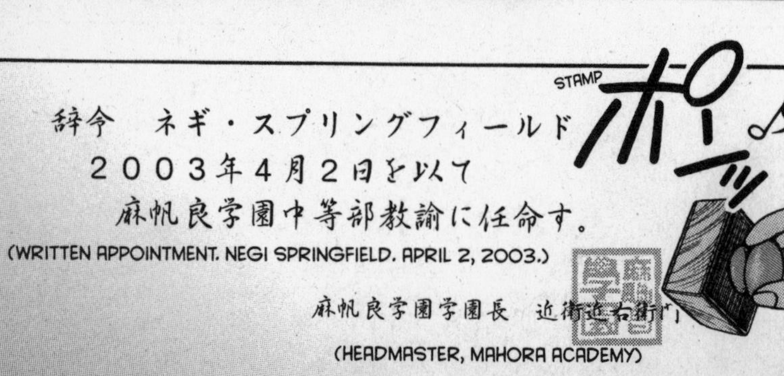
STAMP
辞令　ネギ・スプリングフィールド
２００３年４月２日を以て
麻帆良学園中等部教諭に任命す。
(WRITTEN APPOINTMENT. NEGI SPRINGFIELD. APRIL 2, 2003.)
麻帆良学園学園長　近衛近右衛門
(HEADMASTER, MAHORA ACADEMY)

2A STUDENT PROFILE

STUDENT NUMBER 25
CHISAME HASEGAWA

BORN: FEBRUARY 2, 1989
BLOOD TYPE: B
LIKES: SMALL AND EFFICIENT MACHINES
(SUBNOTEBOOK COMPUTERS, ETC.)
DISLIKES: NEW INVENTIONS IN FOOD AND SWORDS.
AFFILIATIONS: NONE
NOTE: EYESIGHT 1.2

TROMP TROMP
WHAT A GORGEOUS DAY!
IT'S PERFECT FOR THE END OF SCHOOL CEREMONY.
MORNING NEGI-KUN
NI HAO!
GOOD MORNING!
GOOD MORNING, NEGI-KUN!
MORNING, SAKURAKO-SAN!
GOOD MORNING. UH... HASEGAWA-SAN!
CHIRP CHIRP
WHOA, YOU REMEMBERED CHISAME-CHAN, ONE OF THE QUIETEST STUDENTS IN 2-A. THAT'S THE EYE OF A TEACHER!
MORNIN.
WELL... UM...
......
CAN'T BELIEVE THEY'RE RUNNING WHEN THEY'RE NOT EVEN LATE. THIS USED TO BE A NICE, LAZY CLASS.
IT'S ALL THAT SQUIRT'S FAULT.

3RD SEMESTER COMMENCEMENT CEREMONY.
CHATTER
ザワザワ
HO HUMMM. AT THIS TIME, I WISH TO CONGRATULATE NEGI SPRINGFIELD -SENSEI, WHO WILL BE STARTING THIS COMING ACADEMIC YEAR AS A FULL ENGLISH TEACHER.
CHATTER CLATTER
ザワ ザワ…
NEGI-SENSEI WILL TAKE OVER 3-A STARTING IN APRIL.
CLAP CLAP
パチ パチ
CLAP CLAP
パチ パチ
YEAH!
オオーーッ♡
SAY... WHAT!?
WHAT...

TWELFTH PERIOD: EGIRL LIFE.
NEGIMA!

中等部二年A組
(JUNIOR HIGH DEPARTMENT - SECOND YEAR, GROUP A)
SO ALL YOU 2-A STUDENTS...
ペこっ
BOW
I'LL BE SEEING YOU WHEN YOU BECOME 3-A NEXT YEAR!
LOOKING FORWARD TO IT, NEGI-KUN!
SENSEI, OVER HERE! LOOK OVER HERE!
CHECK THIS OUT! THE TROPHY FOR TOP GRADE OF THE YEAR!
YEAH! AND WE OWE IT ALL TO NEGI!
WELL, UH... THAT'S REAL OPTIMISTIC...
IT'S MORE THAN OPTIMISTIC! IT'S GOING TO BE FACT!
WITH NEGI-SENSEI HERE, WE'RE A LOCK TO BE TOPS ON THE MIDTERM TEST.
2-A RALLIED 'ROUND NEGI-SENSEI, AND WE WENT FROM WORST TO FIRST!
AS CLASS REP, I SAY CONGRATULATIONS TO ALL, AND MORE...

ON BEHALF OF US ALL, I KNOW YOU'LL CONTINUE TO WATCH OUT FOR US IN THE FUTURE.
スッ…
BOW
OF... OF COURSE I WILL.
ワイワイ
CHATTER CLATTER
アハハ
AH HA HA

HE BETTER WATCH OUT FOR ME, IS WHAT HE SHOULD DO!
THAT BRAT DID NOTHING, EXCEPT SLACK OFF ON HIS LESSONS EVERY DAY.

WHY IS SOME TEN-YEAR-OLD RUNT IN CHARGE?!
THAT'S GOTTA BE A LABOR LAW VIOLATION!? SOMEONE SHOULD REPORT IT.

TEACHER? I HAVE A QUESTION.
WHAT IS IT, NARU-TAKI-SAN?

ISN'T IT KIND OF ABNORMAL TO HAVE A TEN-YEAR-OLD TEACHER? I'M JUST SAYING.
ざわ…
CHATTER
WHAT'S THIS!?

ALL RIGHT! THOSE SLANTY EYED TWINS AND I ARE ON THE SAME WAVE-LENGTH.
KEEP TALKING.
WELL ...
WELL, FUMIKA AND I THOUGHT WE SHOULD TELL...

...EVERYBODY HOW PROUD WE ARE BY THROWING A "CONGRATS TO THE TOP CLASS" PARTY TODAY!
THAT'S A GREAT IDEA!
EVERY-ONE WHO'S FREE,
GATHER ON THE DORMITORY LAWN!
SHOCK
PLOP
OKAY, THAT DIDN'T GO THE WAY I'D HOPED.
YEAH!
I CAN'T PARTY WITH THESE HAPPY IDIOTS. MY HEAD WILL EXPLODE OR SOMETHING!
SHAKE
HUH?
YOU'RE TREMBLING, HASEGAWA-SAN? DO YOU HAVE CHILLS?
UGH
......
NO.
TWITCH
I'M FINE. JUST... FINE...
SQUIRM
ACTUALLY, NO, MY STOMACH HURTS. I'M OUTTA HERE.
WHA... UH, WAIT A SECOND.
STORM

THIS CLASS HAS BEEN STRANGE FROM THE BEGINNING

GOING ALL THE WAY BACK TO FIRST YEAR.

THERE'S ALL THESE EXCHANGE STUDENTS, COMING IN ONE AFTER THE OTHER.

UNDER-AGE ONES AT THAT, LIKE WE'RE SOME BIG PRE-SCHOOL.

STORM

AND THAT GIRL... SHE'S OBVIOUSLY A ROBOT!

THIS PART IS ROBOTIC.

LIKE THIS PART.

I MEAN, HOW CAN NO ONE ELSE NOTICE? YOU LOOK AT HER AND SAY, "ROBOT!" SHE'S GOTTA BE!

WHAT'S THE PROBLEM, "SENSEI."
I, UH... THOUGHT YOU HAD THE PROBLEM. YOUR STOMACH, Y'KNOW.
HOW DID HE GET HERE SO FAST? HE DIDN'T TAKE A TRAIN FROM THE SCHOOL.

I HAVE THIS GREAT STOMACH-ACHE MEDICINE MY GRAND-FATHER GAVE ME.
I CAN GIVE YOU SOME IF YOU WANT. IT WORKS GREAT.

JEEEEZ, WHAT AN IDIOT...
NO THANKS. I FEEL BETTER ALREADY.

OH! SO... YOU CAN COME TO THE PARTY, THEN!
I'M THINKING NOT. I DON'T DO WELL PARTYING WITH THOSE LUNATICS.
NOW IF YOU'LL EXCUSE ME...

"LUNATICS?" I... THOUGHT THEY WERE KIND OF NORMAL, ACTU—
WELL YOU WOULD, WOULDN'T YOU?! BEING THE HEAD LOON AND ALL!
IRK IRK
イライラ...

UH OH. NOT GOOD. I'M STILL SHAKING...
JITTER

IF YOU'RE FEELING BETTER, WHY'RE YOU STILL TREM-BLING?!
I'M NOT! GO AWAY.
ARE YOU, LIKE, AN ALCOHOLIC OR SOME-THING!?
OH FOR THE LOVE OF--
TROMP TROMP

SLAM
OH...
AH...
SNAP
AAAAHHHHH!!!
SMACK
THIS ISN'T RIGHT.
NORMAL SCHOOLS AREN'T LIKE THIS!
I'LL... I'LL GO OUT INTO THE WORLD...
TELL EVERYONE ABOUT THIS... OUTRAGE-OUSNESS!
THAT SQUIRT THINKS THE OTHERS LOVE HIM.
I'LL SHOW HIM WHAT IS IT TO BE LOVED.
WHOOSH
GLEAM
POUND
LET'S DO IT!

ANOTHER DAY OF CHIU BEING BEAUTIFUL!
OK!
CHISAME REFERS TO HERSELF AS CHIU ON THE NET.
BEEP
WINDOWS THEME
ちうのホームページ
WWW.CHI-U.CO.JP
(CHIU'S HOMEPAGE)
Chiu's Net idol informa
WHOOSH
マンガ
アニメ
ゲーム
ETC.
プロフィール
日記
掲示板
チャット
リンク
Copyright(c)2003 Chiu All Rights Reserved

OH, HELLO. HOW IS EVERYBODY!?
TICK TICK
TODAY, A TERRIBLE THING HAPPENED.
THE TEACHER OF MY CLASS IS A PERVERT!!
LACKEDY CLACK
HE MADE EYES AT CHIU.
CLACK

ちうファンHIRO ＞ 許せねぇ！何だその男？！ (2003/3/25-14:04:25)
CHIU-FAN-HIRO> THAT'S INEXCUSABLE! WHAT'S THE MATTER WITH HIM!
通りすがりB ＞ 俺らがブチのめしてやろうか、ちうタン。(w (2003/3
PASSERBYB> I'D REALLY LIKE TO BEAT HIM UP.
アイスワールド ＞ でも気持ちは分かるよな～。ちうタン美人だし～
ICEWORLD> I TOTALLY GET WHY HE DID. IT'S BECAUSE YOU'RE SO PRETTY...
そうだね～(*^o^*)。ネットアイドルの中では一番綺
CHIU-FAN-HIRO> EXACTLY. THE PRETTIEST OUT OF ALL THE INTERNET IDOLS.

AW, GET OUT! REALLY?
SMIRK

SSSHHH
NORMALLY, I'M AN UNNOTICED, FEMALE JUNIOR HIGH STUDENT! BUT SECRETLY...
I'M THE UMBER ONE DOL ON THE INTERNET, ADORED BY HACKERS EVERYWHERE!
GLEAM
SNAP SNAP
I TAKE PICTURES OF MYSELF WITH A DIGITAL CAMERA!
CLACK
CLICK
THEN I PHOTOSHOP MY SKIN. GET RID OF PIMPLES AND SUCH!
I UPLOAD THE PHOTOS WITH FTP!
AND THE GUYS GO NUTS FOR ME!
I FEEL CHARMING! OH, SO CHARMING!
IT'S ALARMING HOW CHARMING I FEEL!

YUP! I'VE STILL GOT IT!
TAH DAH
RANKED NUMBER ONE BY A MILE!
I'M QUEEN OF THE NET! MORE CHARISMA THAN ANYONE ELSE, EVER!
ALL MEN KNEEL BEFORE ME!
LLAAAAA
AND THAT FREAK KID TEACHER WILL DO THE SAME.
?
HE THINKS HE'S A MATCH FOR ME? HAH!
IN THE "REAL" WORLD, I'M HARMLESS. NO THREAT TO ANYONE.
BUT IN THE WORLD "BEHIND THE SCENES," I'VE REACHED THE TOP.
HUH?
......
UH, EXCUSE ME. THE DOOR WAS OPEN SO I...
GASP

HE...HE'S SEEN ME!?!
THAT BRAT KNOWS MY SECRET!?

IT'S RUINED! ALL RUINED!
?
HE'LL TELL EVERYONE I'M AS CRAZY AS THEY ARE, WITH MY PRANCING AROUND IN A BUNNY-SUIT FOR INTERNET-GLORY! THEY'LL LAUGH THEIR BUTTS OFF!

WELCOME TO THE CRAZY GROUP 2-A!
WELCOME CRAZY PERSON!
I HAVE TO VANISH. IT'S THE ONLY THING LEFT.
BUT FIRST I KILL HIM. MY FINAL REVENGE. I NEED A SHARP INSTRUMENT... OR BLUNT. BLUNT IS GOOD, TOO.
STAGGER

WHOA, HASEGAWA-SAN! IS THAT YOU? YOU LOOK GORGEOUS IN THIS PICTURE.
WOBBLE
UH...

WELL... NATURALLY. I MEAN, I AM THE INTERNET'S TOP IDOL!
I JUST USED MY SKILLS TO ENHANCE THE IMAGE, THAT'S ALL.
WELL WELL
DIDN'T TAKE MUCH WORK, THOUGH.
YOINK
ひょい...
WHA-!?

HEY, MY GLASSES!
ARRG
I MEAN, YOU STARTED WITH SUCH A BEAUTIFUL FACE, SO IT DIDN'T NEED MUCH TO "PRETTY IT UP."
WHAT!?
FLUSTER
AHEM
SO C'MON, HASEGAWA-SAN.
COME TO THE PARTY ON THE LAWN BELOW. EVERYONE'S THERE!
HEY! GIMME BACK MY GLASSES!
HA HA. NO WAY.
SIZZLE
SOMEONE SO PRETTY SHOULDN'T HIDE BEYOND SUCH HUGE SPECS.
BUT I CAN'T SEE WITHOUT THEM!
CLATTER
AND I HATE PARTIES! AND PEOPLE! BEING WITH THEM, I MEAN! GIMME THOSE BACK!
OH, REALLY? C'MON!
MAKE AN EXCEPTION, JUST FOR TODAY!

JUST LOOK!
THE DAY'S ALMOST AS BEAUTIFUL AS YOU!
'MON!
......
AS BEAUTIFUL AS THAT?
......
WELL, OK.
MAYBE HANGING OUT WITH THE CRAZIES FOR ONE DAY WON'T HURT.

ワイワイ
CHATTER
アハハ
SORRY WE'RE LATE.
WAIT, YOU IDIOT! I NEED TO GO BACK AND- CHANGE FIRST-!
HOW'D HE GET SO STRONG?
WHO'S THAT WITH SENSEI!
IT'S SOME CUTE GIRL!
SHE MAKES THAT OUTFIT WORK, THOUGH!
HEH HEH HEH.
SENSEI BROUGHT A DATE? WOW.
かわいー!
HOW CUTE!
A BUNNY!
IT'S A BUNNY!
DON'T YOU GET IT? SENSEI'S DATING A PLAYBOY BUNNY! WAY TO GO, SENSEI!
キャー
AHH
ガヤガヤ
HUBBUB
WHAT...
WAIT A...
カァァー
ACK!

WAAAAIT A SECOND, NEGI. IS THAT...?
SENSEI! GIVE ME MY GLASSES BACK.
HUH!?
GRASP
WHISP
HAIR'S PERFUMED! I'M GONNA—
HUH?
KAH...
KAH...
NOT THIS AGAIN!
AACK!
KAH-CHOO!

HUH?
ハラ
STUN
WHAT?
ハラ
STUN
WHAT TH–?
OOOOHHHH! THE BUNNY COSTUME TRANS-FORMS INTO A FLOWER PETAL?
. . . . .
オオーー
OOOH AAAHH
THAT'S A GREAT TRICK!
PRETTY IMPRES-SIVE, NEGI-SENSEI!
HOLD IT! THAT'S HASEGAWA!?
UH-UH-UH...
NO, NO WAY!
IT REALLY IS CHISAME-CHAN!
キャーキャー
YIKES!
YOU'RE WRONG! I DON'T KNOW ANY HASEGAWA! I'M NOT HER, NO WAY!
CHISAME-CHAN'S AN EXHIBI-TIONIST!
I'LL KILL HIM. SOMEHOW, SOME WAY, I'LL KILL HIM.
S-SORRY.
ポコッ
BONK

STUDENT NUMBER 22
FUKA NARUTAKI (RIGHT)

BORN: DECEMBER 6, 1988
BLOOD TYPE: A
LIKES: PRANKS, SWEET THINGS
DISLIKES: GHOSTS, KEEPING QUIET
AFFILIATIONS: STROLLING CLUB
NOTE: EYESIGHT 1.2

STUDENT NUMBER 23
FUMIKA NARUTAKI (LEFT)

BORN: DECEMBER 6, 1988
BLOOD TYPE: A
LIKES: CLEANING, SWEET THINGS
DISLIKES: LONG, HAIRY THINGS (LIKE CATERPILLARS)
AFFILIATIONS: STROLLING CLUB, BEAUTIFICATION COMMITTEE

NEGIMA!
THIRTEENTH PERIOD:
RECOMMENDED!
THE CHILD STROLLING BRIGADE

NEGI-KUN!
HEY! NEGI-BOZU!
WHERE'D HE GET OFF TO?
FIRST HE SAID HE WANTED TO REALLY TOUR THE ACADEMY, SINCE WE'VE GOT THE TIME DURING SPRING BREAK... AND NOW HE'S GONE!
MAYBE HE WANDERED OFF AND GOT LOST.
YO! ASAKURA! GOOD TIMING!
CAN YOU DELIVER A MESSAGE FOR US?
SCREETCH
OH!
WHAT A GORGEOUS DAY! HEY, ASUNA, WHAT WOULD YOU SAY TO A PICNIC?
I'D SAY, "GO AWAY, PICNIC, I WANNA GO HOME AND SLEEP."
帰って寝たいし…
KILLJOY. YOU SHOULD JOIN THE STROLLING CLUB.
CHIRP CHIRP
チチチ…

WOW! I NEVER REALIZED HOW BEAUTIFUL THE GROUNDS AT MAHORA ACADEMY REALLY ARE.
DING DONG GONG!
LOST CHILD AN-NOUNCE-MENT!
NEGI SPRINGFIELD FROM THE JUNIOR HIGH DEPARTMENT ENGLISH DIVISION.
YOUR GUARDIANS ARE WAITING NEAR THE OBSERVATORY.
WHA--? BUT I'M A TEACHER!
NEGI-SENSEI IS A LOST CHILD!?
HAH HAH
NOT FUNNY, ASUNA-SAN!
NOT TO YOU, MAYBE...
WE JUST WANTED TO MAKE SURE YOU HURRIED BACK.
I'M SORRY, OKAY? WELL... NOT REALLY...
ALL WILL BE FORGIVEN. CHECK THIS OUT.
WOW!!
THIS... THIS IS MAGNIFICENT!

TO THE RIGHT IS THE RESIDENTIAL DISTRICT AND OUR DORM.
STRAIGHT UP THE HILL ARE THE UNIVERSITY FACILITIES AND RESEARCH INSTITUTES.
IT'S... IT'S LIKE IT GOES ON FOREVER!
WE STICK MAINLY TO THE AREA AROUND THE JUNIOR HIGH DIVISION.
IT'S MAIL FROM MY GRAND-FATHER!
HE HAS A JOB FOR ASUNA AND ME.
HUH!?
OK, YOU GO ON THEN. I'LL BE FINE EXPLORING ON MY OWN. REALLY.

← ON THE LEFT, IS THE OLDER SISTER, FUKA-CHAN. ON THE RIGHT, IS THE YOUNGER SISTER, FUMIKA.

← YUNA AKASHI. NUMBER 2.

ピッ ピッ
WHISTLE
ワイ ワイ
BUMP BUMP
THIS IS THE JUNIOR HIGH DIVISION'S EXCLUSIVE GYM.
OH!
WE WORK UP A SWEAT IN TWENTY-ONE FITNESS-RELATED CLUBS.
I HEAR THE ONLY CLUBS WHO REALLY HAVE GAMES ARE THE VOLLEYBALL AND DODGEBALL CLUBS.
IS THAT RIGHT?
ALSO, THE GIRLY RHYTHMIC GYMNASTICS ARE GOOD.
BUT THE BASKETBALL CLUB IS PRETTY WEAK.
BASKETBALL CLUB
HEY! CUT IT OUT!
INDEED. IT'S GOOD THAT FEMALE STUDENTS ARE TRYING HARD AT SPORTS.
さわやかだなー
IT'S REFRESHING.
WOW, SENSEI, YOU SOUND LIKE AN OLD MAN.
HUH! FIRST I'M A CHILD, NOW I'M AN "OLD MAN?!"
BUT YOU KNOW WHAT I MEAN.
おませさん♡
I'M JUST MESSING WITH YOU.
WANT TO CHECK OUT THE LOCKER ROOM? I KNOW YOU'VE BEEN DYING TO.
更衣室
おねーちゃ…
SIS-SISTER.
TEE HEE HEE♡
OH! IT'S NEGI-KUN.
OKAY, THAT IS SO NOT HAPPENING!

THIS IS THE INDOOR POOL.
SPLASH
WHISTLE
OH, THAT'S RIGHT. THE SWIM TEAM IS PRETTY STRONG.
AKIRA, FROM OUR CLASS, IS INCREDIBLY FAST.
AKIRA OKOCHI. NUMBER 6.
AKIRA!
HE- HELLO.
HELLO, NEGI-SENSEI.
SO THIS IS THE FAMOUS KID TEACHER!
VERY, UH... MODEST SWIMSUITS. AND... TIGHT...
OH.
AH HA HA
CHATTER
THIS KID CAN REALLY TEACH?
HARD TO BE- LIEVE.
GIGGLE
HEE HEE HEE
TEE HEE. HE DOESN'T KNOW WHICH WAY TO LOOK.
IT'S TOUGH BECAUSE THERE'S SO MANY, THEY'RE ALWAYS SCRAMBLING FOR COURT SPACE.
THIS IS WHERE THE OUTDOOR ATHLETIC CLUBS WORK OUT.
WHISK

LOOK WHO'S COME TO WATCH! NEGI-KUN!
HE'S CHECKING YOU OUT, SAKURAKO.
OH, LIKE THESE OUTFITS ARE MADE TO DIS-COURAGE STARES.
......
HEY! SENSEI'S FINALLY STUCK FOR WORDS!
ALL THIS SEXINESS MAKE YOU NERVOUS?
NO, BUT YOUR DETERMINATION TO SHOW IT TO ME DOES!
AAH, SENSEI'S PISSED.
OH, IT IS SO YOUR FAULT!
IT'S NOT MY FAULT THIS IS A GIRL'S SCHOOL!
TROMP TROMP
SORRY WE COULDN'T COVER THE WHOLE CULTURE DEPART-MENT IN ONE DAY.
AFTER ALL, THERE'S 160 CLUBS, SO...
WHAT SORTA SCHOOL IS THIS!?
WHEEZ
GASP
I'M STARVED. WHO WANTS TO GRAB A SNACK?
I'M GAME.
SINCE YOU'RE IN CHARGE, IT'S YOUR TREAT! RIGHT, SENSEI?
FROM UNDER-GROUND TO THE ROOF, THE CAFETERIA HAS EVERY KIND OF FOOD.

AH, THIS MANGO PUDDING CHOCOLATE PARFAIT IS DELICIOUS!
IT'S THIS MONTH'S NEW CREATION.
SORRY TO KEEP YOU WAITING.
YOU GUYS SURE CAN EAT.
¥380
HEY! SENSEI. OPEN WIDE.
GIGGLE くすくす♡
SURE, WHY NOT.
CHATTER キャイキャイ♡
THESE TWINS ARE SOMETHING ELSE.
BUT THEY'RE EASIER TO TALK TO THAN SOME OF THEIR CLASSMATES.
IT'S PROBABLY BECAUSE THEY'RE SHORTER THAN ME... AND KIND OF IMMATURE.
ANYA'S ALSO LIKE THAT.
IT'S LIKE MY OLDER SISTER ALWAYS SAID:
YOU CAN'T JUDGE A BOOK BY ITS COVER.
I WONDER WHAT THE JAPANESE EQUIVALENT FOR THAT WOULD BE...?
WHAT'RE YOU WRITING, NEGI-SENSEI?
IT'S NOTHING! NOTHING.
OOOO-OKAY...
WELL, UH...
PROBABLY TIME TO CALL IT A DAY. IT'LL BE EVENING SOON, SO...
OH, NO, SENSEI, DON'T SAY THAT YET!
RIGHT! THERE'S ONE VERY IMPORTANT PLACE LEFT.

GASP WHEEZ
THIS SORTA PLACE IS BEHIND THE MOUNTAIN?
JUST A LITTLE FURTHER, SENSEI! HOLD ON!
I CAN SEE IT FROM HERE!
OH.
I'VE SEEN GLIMPSES OF THIS TREE FROM ALL OVER CAMPUS! IT'S HUGE!
SUPPOSEDLY IT'S BEEN HERE SINCE BEFORE THE ACADEMY WAS BUILT.
IT'S CALLED THE WORLD TREE.
UH... THE WORLD TREE?
SENSEI, YOU DON'T KNOW OF MARUE DORA? ABOUT HOW SHE CAME BACK TO LIFE AS THE WORLD TREE?
SIS, OF COURSE HE HASN'T HEARD OF HER. HE'S BRITISH.

THERE'S SEVERAL LEGENDS ABOUT THIS TREE.
YOU OFTEN HEAR OF THEM.
ONE SAYS THAT IF YOU TELL SOMEONE YOU HAVE A CRUSH ON THAT YOU LIKE THEM,
IT WILL COME TRUE.
PRETTY ROMANTIC, HUH?
YEP.
EVEN THOUGH THEY SEEM CHILDISH...
THEY'RE ACTUALLY RESPECTABLE GIRLS.
A CRUSH, HUH. MAYBE I...

ANYA...
HMMM
SISTER...
LORD, NO...
KONOKA-SAN...
GLARE
HUH!
OH, NO FREAKING WAY. BESIDES, TEACHERS AND STUDENTS... IT'S JUST WRONG.
FUMIKA, I'VE AN IDEA!
LET'S TELL SENSEI WE LIKE HIM, AND MAYBE... JUST FOR A LITTLE WHILE... HE'LL BE OUR BOYFRIEND!
COME AGAIN!?
AH, GOOD IDEA. THE WORLD TREE WILL CERTAINLY MAKE THAT COME TRUE.
NO! TOTAL OPPOSITE OF GOOD IDEA! A TEACHER MUST NEVER TAKE ADVANTAGE OF A STUDENT'S FEELINGS... SO... YOU SHOULDN'T, EVEN IN JEST...
ACK!
AH!
EEYEAH
NO WAY. YOU'RE NOT GETTING AWAY. FUKA, GRAB HIM OVER THERE!
AAH! WHAT HAPPENS IF THAT STUPID LEGEND'S TRUE?!
HEH HEH HEH
CLASP
CLASP
ALL TOGETHER NOW.
OH.
SMOOCH

WE LOVE NEGI-SENSEI!
PLEASE TREAT US AGAIN TO PUDDING AND PARFAIT!
AH!
UGH... I'M A TEACHER BUT EVERYONE TREATS ME LIKE A CHILD.
I'M GONNA REDO THIS. THOSE GIRLS ARE THE SMART ALECKS.
パラ
パラ
RUFFLE
ガチャ…
BANG
HEY, NEGI! WE'RE BACK.
HOW WAS THE TWIN'S TOUR OF THE ACADEMY?
HUH?
愛媛
みかん
ドキ…
SHOCK
UH... FINE. FINE. TOTALLY, Y'KNOW... FINE.
WHAT'S WRONG WITH YOU? IF YOUR FACE LOOKED ANY MORE RED, YOU'D BE SUNBURNED.
あわわっ
OH NO NO
WHAT ARE YOU WRITING ON THE CLASS ROSTER, NEGI-KUN?

21. CHIZURU NABA
ASTRONOMY CLUB
MORE OF A DANGO THAN A FLOWER
VERY ADULT-LIKE.
FUKA TWINS
22. FUKA NARUTAKI
WALKING CLUB
(NON-S
22. FUKA NARU
WALKING CLUB
OLDER SISTER
RE IN TROUBLE
FUMIKA
SURPRISINGLY SKILLED
23. FUMIKA NARUTAKI
SCHOOL DECOR CLUB
WALKING CLUB
BOTH OF THEM ARE STILL CHILDREN
KA MIYAZAKI

WHAT!? VERY A-ADULT-LIKE!?
JAW DROP
SURPRISINGLY SK-SKILLED!?
GAPE

2A STUDENT PROFILE

STUDENT NUMBER 29
AYAKA YUKIHIRO

BORN: JULY 5, 1988
BLOOD TYPE: O
LIKES: NEGI-SENSEI, FLOWERS, PURE AND INNOCENT BOYS
DISLIKES: VIOLENT AND DISORDERLY PEOPLE
AFFILIATIONS: EQUESTRIAN CLUB, FLOWER ARRANGEMENT CLUB
NOTES: SECOND DAUGHTER OF THE YUKIHIRO ZAIBATSU, OWNER OF A BUSINESS MONOPOLY FORMED DURING WAR TIME. BEAUTIFUL APPEARANCE, CLEAR-HEADED (RANKED 4TH), IS MADLY IN LOVE WITH NEGI-SENSEI.

NEGIMA!
FOURTEENTH PERIOD:
YESTERDAY'S ENEMY IS
TOMORROW'S NEMESIS

OKAY, CLASS.
THIS IS OUR NEW STUDENT, ASUNA KAGU-RAZAKA.
JINGLE
チリン…
SHE TRANSFERRED HERE FROM OVERSEAS. SO PLEASE...
MAKE HER FEEL WELCOME.
かぐらざか あすなちゃん
WE WILL!
はーい♡
......
......
HUH?
GONG
DONG
DING
WAIT A MINUTE! YOU, WITH THE ATTITUDE AND EVIL EYE!
YOU LOOK PRETTY COCKY FOR A SMALL-FRY TRANSFER STUDENT!
......
HUH? WHAT'S THAT YOU SAY?

I SAID, "SHRIMP!"
PPRAWR
ブチッ
WHA- ?
HOW DARE YOU! YOU'RE NOT A SMALL-FRY! YOU'RE A BRAT!
FIGHT'S STARTED!
FRACAS
ドタバタ
......!
WHO'S CALLING WHO A SMALL FRY?! YOU IDIOT!
I'VE GOT 10 YEN ON THE CLASS REP!
FIVE YEN ON THE NEW GIRL!
SHRIEK
キャキャ
THEY'RE FIRST YEAR STUDENTS SO THEY'RE BOTH SHRIMPS!
AH...
AHHH! THAT LITTLE BRAT!!
PANT PANT
ARGH.

GOOD MORNING, EVERYONE.
GOOD MORNING, HONORABLE OJOU-SAMA.
HMM, MY TEA PLEASE.
RIGHT AWAY, OJOU-SAMA.
ANOTHER WORTHLESS DREAM THIS MORNING.
AND EACH ONE STARS THAT VIOLENT CRETIN, ASUNA.
I CAN'T EVEN LEAVE HER BEHIND FOR SPRING BREAK.
SOME LOUSY DAY THIS IS GONNA BE...
IRK
IRK
OJOU-SAMA, A CHILD CALLED PRETENDING TO BE YOUR TEACHER.
A CHI--? WAIT! NE-NEGI-SENSEI!?
DID HE LEAVE A MESSAGE?
YES. I THOUGHT IT APROPOS TO WRITE IT IN CRAYON.

EEYAH! YES!
IT SAYS HE'S COMING HERE! TO VISIT! ASAP!
CHUCKLE
ハッハッハ
YAY! HA HA. YES! I'VE DONE IT! THE PERFECT DAY OFF, AND I'VE GOT JUST THE DRESS TO SHOW OFF!
くるくる
TWIRL
WE'RE INTO WEIRD TERRITORY NOW.
NO KIDDING.
AH
ハッ
UM...
UM, OJOU-SAMA...
WHEN MY TEACHER ARRIVES, BE RESPECTFUL!
AHEM
コホーン
OH.
CER-TAINLY.
YES MA' AM.
AH, LOOK AT THAT SKY..
PERFECT FOR A DAY OUT.
......
WHOA......

THAT'S NOT A HOUSE, THAT'S WINDSOR CASTLE!
NE-NEGI-SENSEI!
WELCOME! MAKE YOURSELF AT HOME.
ARGH!
SKID
TH-THANK YOU.
HI YA, CLASS REP.
DRESSED KINDA FANCY FOR ROLLING ON THE GROUND, AINT'CHA?

WHAT... WHAT'S ASUNA DOING HERE FOR THE LOVE OF–
CALM DOWN.
I COULD ASK YOU WHY YOU'RE WEARING SUCH A GET-UP.
WE'RE HIS GUARDIANS. WE'RE, Y'KNOW... GUARDING HIM.
IF WE LET HIM GO ALONE, WHO KNOWS WHAT YOU'D DO WITH HIM.
GRRR
WELL, SURE! AFTER ALL I MIGHT DO SOME-THING...
...LIKE THIS! OR THIS!!! OR–
POW
BAM
O-OJOU-SAMA! EVERYONE WILL SEE YOU.
SMACK
THAT'S IT! SHE'S COMPLETELY SNAPPED!
ASUNA! ASUNA!
STOP OR I'M LEAVING!
THERE, THAT'S BETTER. WOW, WHAT A LARGE GARDEN!
THAT'S ONLY THE FRONT YARD.
WELL, NEGI-SENSEI.
TO WHAT DO I OWE THE HONOR OF YOUR VISIT?

WELL, UM... TODAY IS...
YEAH, WELL...
I JUST FIGURED, Y'KNOW...I SHOULD GET O KNOW THE CLASS REP BETTER.
AH... REALLY!?
WELL, THAT'S ...
AHH, I COULDN'T BE HAPPIER, NEGI-SENSEI. IN... IN FACT...
DIZZY
くらくら
IT'S DIZZYING, ALL THIS HAPPINESS...
STAGGER
よろろっ...
あの…
UH...
OF COURSE, IT'S NOT AS IF I EXPECTED YOU TO SAY, "LET ME WHISPER SWEET NOTHINGS IN YOUR EAR. WE COULD HAVE A DEEP, INTIMATE RELATIONSHIP." THAT SORT OF THING.
PANT PANT
ハァハァ
STROKE PAT
なでなで
LISTEN TO OURSELF! HAT'S THE MATTER ITH YOU?!
CARE TO SEE MY BEDROOM? OF COURSE YOU WOULD.
?
SHE'S FAST, GIVE HER THAT.
YO! OLITA! IAL IT OWN!
THIS IS MY PRIVATE ROOM.
WOW! IT'S HUGE!

YUP, I REMEMBER THIS VIEW FROM WHEN WE WERE IN ELEMENTARY SCHOOL.
PLEASE, GIRLS, DON'T FEEL OBLIGED TO BE ANYWHERE ELSE IN THIS HOUSE. ESPECIALLY YOU, ASUNA.
DO YOU LIKE HERBAL TEA, NEGI-SENSEI?
UH, YEAH.
FOR YOU, NEGI-SENSEI, I HAVE TEAS FROM AROUND THE WORLD. YOU CAN HAVE ANYTHING YOU SEE HERE... AND I MEAN *ANYTHING.*
パチン SNAP
すっ JUMP
ガラガラ RATTLE
FROM THE RIGHT WE HAVE ROSE HIP, LEMON VERBENA, DANDELION, GERMAN CHAMOMILE, SWEET FENNEL, ELDER-FLOWER, ST. JOHN'S WORT, LINDEN, AND SAGE.
UM, THANK YOU.
ANY HEMLOCK?
HAVE YOUR PICK OF TEA BISCUITS, SENSEI.
THERE'S CHOCOLATE COOKIES AND OTHER FAMOUS SWEETS FROM AROUND THE WORLD.
ガラガラ CLANK CLANK
WHOAH!
ドドサーッ CRASH
REP, THIS IS A BIT MUCH, EVEN FOR YOU.
IT'S DELICIOUS, CLASS REP-SAN.
REMINDS ME OF THE PARFAITS MY SISTER ALWAYS MADE.
UH...
YOU HAVE A SISTER?
OKAY, LET'S LEAVE SCARLET O'HARLOT BE FOR NOW AND GO SWIMMING. IF I REMEMBER RIGHT, THE POOL'S OUT THIS WAY...
AND IT'S GORGEOUS. YOU IN, NEGI-KUN?
OH, YEAH! ABSOLUTELY!
HEY! WAIT A SECOND! I HAVE MANY OTHER TREATS TO SERVE NEGI-SENSEI!

YAHOO!!
YOU GOTTA BE KID-DING.
SPLASH
NEGI-KUN! REP! WHO'S UP FOR A RACE!
NO WAY. ASUNA SWIMS FASTER THAN FLIPPER.
THAT'S BECAUSE SHE MOVES VERY PORPOISE-FULLY! HA HA HA. AHH.. UM.
AHEM. YES, SHE'S VERY ENER-GETIC.
AND IMMATURE. WHEREAS YOU, NEGI-SENSEI, ALL OF TEN YEARS OLD, ARE SO ADULT IN COMPARISON.
RUB
UH, WELL... THAT'S ...

BOTH ASUNA-SAN AND KONOKA-SAN HAVE BEEN LIKE THAT SINCE WE WERE IN ELEMENTARY SCHOOL.

BUT WHEN ASUNA FIRST TRANSFERRED HERE, SHE WAS QUIETER.

WOW, YOU'VE BEEN FRIENDS SINCE ELEMENTARY SCHOOL!

FRIENDS? LIKE HELL!! WE'RE SWORN ENEMIES!!

WE INSULT EACH OTHER'S HOBBIES, SABOTAGE EACH OTHER DURING TESTS OR AT ATHLETIC MEETS.

FOR SEVEN YEARS, WE'VE BEEN CATS AND DOGS, OIL AND WATER, STURM AND DRANG.

THEY'RE DELICIOUS!
THESE ARE GREAT. VERY BUTTERY.
THERE'S LOTS MORE WHERE THOSE CAME FROM.
OK, CONTINUING WITH THE TEA. THIS IS SOMETHING I GREW SO I DON'T KNOW IF IT'S GOOD OR NOT.
OU MADE THIS? WOW, I'M MPRESSED.
......
I'M THE ONLY ONE EATING THEM.
DOES THE CLASS REP WANT SOME?
......
OOOHH, NEGI-SENSEI.
YES?
WHAT IS IT?
......
ウズウズ
BURSTING

抱きっ♡
SQUEEZE
GULP!
むぎゅっ…
SQUISH
AYA...
WHAT!?
NEGI-SENSEI.
にへ
BEAM
I'LL BE YOUR SISTER WHILE YOU'RE HERE!
THAT'S... THAT'S GREAT, REP, BUT...
ムギュウゥ…♡
SQUASH
...BREATHING IS... GETTING...
...PROBLEMATIC...
じたばた
STRUGGLE

*LOLITA: FAMOUSLY OVERSEXED TEEN IN A BOOK BY VLADIMIR NABOKOV.

CLASS REP-SAN.
I TAKE BACK THE CRACK ABOUT YOU BEING A CHILD MOLESTER. JUST FOR TODAY.
I'M SORRY.
A-ASUNA SAN.
GOOD-BYE.
......
IS THAT GONNA DO IT ASUNA?
WE'LL BE FINE.
I APOLOGIZE NEGI-SENSEI.
I SHOULDN'T HAVE SHOWN YOU THAT UGLY SIDE OF ME.
ASUNA AND I ALWAYS FIGHT LIKE THIS.
SHE HATES ME AND I HA—
YOU'RE WRONG.

COMING HERE WASN'T MY IDEA, CLASS REP-SAN. IT WAS ASUNA-SAN'S.
SHE WANTED TO CHEER YOU UP.
WHAT...
CLASS EP-SAN, OU HAD A KID ROTHER BOUT MY AGE, RIGHT?
AH...
MY BROTHER'S GONNA BE BORN REALLY SOON.
AND HE'S GONNA HAVE A GREAT BIG ROOM! AND...
...... AND...
WHAT!?
WHAT DO YOU MEAN I CAN'T SEE HIM!?
......
I'M VERY SORRY, AYAKA.
SOB!
......

WHAT A WASTE OF TOYS
THIS WAS SUPPOSED TO BE HIS ROOM, BUT...
WHIMPER
CHEER UP!
ARGH!
HEE YAH
GET BACK HERE, YOU SHRIMP! I'M GONNA GET YOU!!
JUST FOLLOW THE SOUND OF MY PONY-TAIL BELLS, DEMON!
AT LEAST AYAKA-CHAN IS A LITTLE MORE PEPPY.
THAT'S RIGHT...
TODAY IS MY LITTLE BROTHER'S BIRTHDAY.
I CAN'T BELIEVE ...
SINCE WE WERE LITTLE, SHE ...

SHE'S A VIOLENT, DISORDERLY...
HORRIBLE CLASSMATE.
......
CLASS REP-SAN.
I CAN'T REPLACE YOUR BROTHER IN YOUR HEART... BUT FOR TODAY, I'LL REPLACE HIM IN YOUR HOUSE...
...IF YOU WANT ME TO, THAT IS. WHATEVER YOUR HEART DESIRES.
WHAT-EVER MY HEART DESIRES?
YES, WHAT-EVER YOUR HEART ESIRES.
HEH HEH HEH.
THANK YOU, NEGI-SENSEI.

I'M BACK.

WELCOME HOME NEGI-KUN. DID EVERYTHING GO OKAY?

WHAT DID THE CLASS REP SAY?

SHE SAID SOMETHING LIKE "SORRY."

AH... IS THAT RIGHT.

......

HEH HEH

WHISK

EMERGENCY CONTACT (PRIMARY)

ASUNA'S CLOSE FRIEND.

29. AYAKA YUKIHIRO
CLASS REPRESENTATIVE
EQUESTRIAN CLUB

25. CHISAME

抱きーっ♡
SQUEEZE

NEGIMA!
FIFTEENTH PERIOD:
NEGI-SENSEI'S WEDDING!?

チャー
SIZZLE
NEW SEMESTER BEGINS TOMORROW! AND ABOUT TIME, TOO!
EGGS SUNNY-SIDE UP, ENGLISH STYLE, FOR THE PRECOCIOUS NEGI-KUN.
pooh!
チャッ
SIZZLE
チャッ♡
SIZZLE
タッ
CLASP
REALLY, NEGI-KUN?
MMMM. WE'VE GOT SOME FREE TIME.
ひょいぱく ひょいぱく
ドタバタ
CLATTER
MUNCH MUNCH
YUM! IT'S DELICIOUS KONOKA-SAN!
YEAH! I'M GLAD.
ASUNA ALWAYS DITCHES ME AFTER SHE EATS.
YUP. I'M EVIL.

REALLY IT'S REALLY GOOD KONOKA-SAN. YOU'LL MAKE A LOVELY WIFE.
YOU'RE TOO MUCH, NEGI-KUN!
FLUSH
CLANK

NOT TOO HEAVY FOR YOU, IS IT?
IT'S FINE.

AS ALWAYS, THANK YOU, NEGI-KUN.
SHUCKS
GOTTA DO SOME-THING TO EARN MY KEEP.

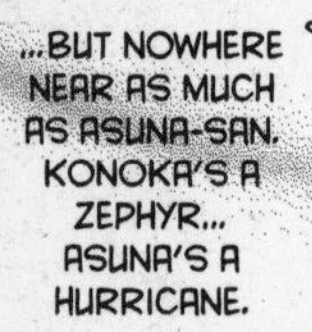

IT'S BEEN A LONG TIME, NEGI.
POOF
ARE YOU WELL?
English
▶Japanese
▶play
WHOA! IT'S FROM MY SISTER.
WOW! A TINY TALKING IMAGE! IT'S AMAZING... SO THAT'S YOUR SIS, HUH?
CONGRATULATIONS ON YOUR BECOMING A RESPECTABLE TEACHER.
HEH HEH
FROM NOW ON, IT'S THE REAL DEAL, SO BE DILIGENT AND DO YOUR BEST.
ALSO... HEH HEH... PERHAPS I'M JUMPING THE GUN, BUT I WONDER IF YOU FOUND YOUR PARTNER?
WIZARDS AND PARTNERS ATTRACT EACH OTHER SO SHE'S ALREADY PROBABLY SOMEONE CLOSE TO YOU.
* GIGGLE *· WHOEVER YOU FIND DURING YOUR APPRENTICESHIP, I HOPE SHE'S LOVELY.
PARTNER?
A PARTNER, HUH?
SIS, IT'S A LITTLE EARLY FOR THAT.
FLUTTER FLUTTER
FLAP
YOU BEEN HOLDING OUT, NEGI! YOU GOT A FIANCÉ SOMEWHERE?
A LOVER? "PRECOCIOUS" AIN'T THE HALF OF IT!
SCRUNCH
NO, NO, NOTHING LIKE THAT!

ACCORDING TO THE OLD STORIES WE WIZARDS PASS DOWN, ONE TO THE NEXT...
IT'S A HUGE SORCERESS WHO SAVES THE WORLD AND THE BRAVE WARRIOR WHO PROTECTS HER.
WHAT'S THAT?
A STATUE IN A COUNTRY PLAZA.
IT'S THE TRADITIONAL HOPE THAT WIZARDS WHO ARE ACTIVE IN SOCIETY WILL FIND A ...FOR WANT OF A BETTER WORD...
MATE WHO WILL, Y'KNOW, WATCH THEIR BACK. SUCH A PARTNER IS CALLED THE "MINISTER MAGI."
IN FACT, YOU CAN'T BE CONSIDERED A MAGISTER MAGI IF YOU HAVE NO PARTNER.
HMMM. A PARTNER.
SO IT'S ALWAYS A MALE/FEMALE PAIRING? IS THAT RIGHT?
YEAH. MEN AND WOMEN HAVE DIFFERENT PRIORITIES, SO THEY COMPLEMENT EACH OTHER. PLUS, Y'KNOW, THE HANDSOME HERO ALWAYS WANTS THE BEAUTIFUL HEROINE, AND VICE VERSA.
HEH HEH
A LOT OF PARTNERS WIND UP MARRYING EACH OTHER.
GRIN
SO I WAS RIGHT THE FIRST TIME: IT'S A LOVER.

SO YOU REALLY CAME TO JAPAN TO FIND A LOVER, NEGI-KUN?
WELL, OUR CLASS ALONE GIVES YOU THIRTY TO CHOOSE FROM.
NO, IT'S NOT LIKE THAT AT ALL.
?
WHAH! KONOKA-SAN!
びっくぅ
SHOCK
KONOKA. WH-WHAT DID YOU HEAR?
THE PART ABOUT FINDING IDEAL PARTNERS. SO WHAT'S IN THAT LETTER?
IT'S NOTHING. NOTHING AT ALL.
HEY EVERYBODY! NEGI-KUN CAME TO JAPAN TO FIND A LOVER!!
ギャー
AAACK!
NO! NO! I REALLY CAME TO BE A TEACHER.
TAKE IT EASY, NEGI-KUN. I WAS JUST JOKING.
ASUNA, MY GRANDFATHER CALLED ME AGAIN, SO I'M OFF.

DOES HE WANT TO TALK TO YOU ABOUT "YOU KNOW" AGAIN?
MAY-BE. SEE YA.
HUH? WHAT'S "YOU KNOW"?
NEVER MIND. BOY, KONOKA SHOWED UP OUTTA NOWHERE.
YEAH, I THOUGHT WORD ABOUT ME WAS OUT FOR SURE.
......
DID YOU HEAR THAT?
バタン
DING
I HEARD IT.

THIS IS BIG!
BIG! IT'S HUGE! NEGI-SENSEI CAME TO JAPAN TO FIND A PARTNER.
TROMP TROMP
WH-WHAT DID YOU SAY!?
NEGI-SENSEI IS LOOKING FOR A PARTNER!?

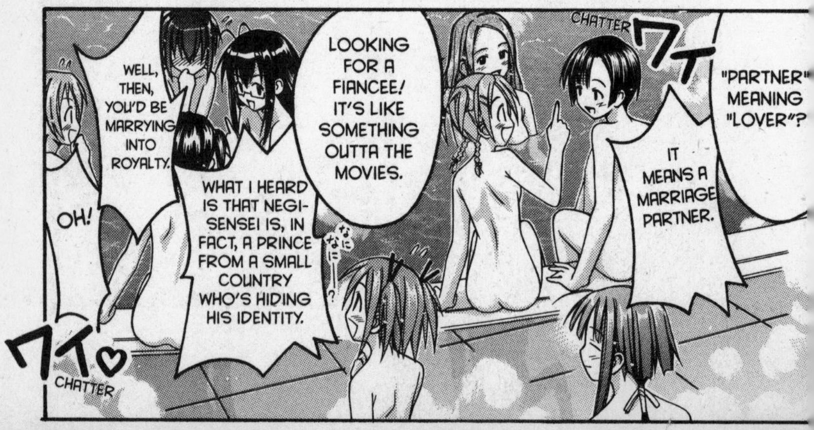
"PARTNER" MEANING "LOVER"?
CHATTER
ワイ
IT MEANS A MARRIAGE PARTNER.
LOOKING FOR A FIANCEE! IT'S LIKE SOMETHING OUTTA THE MOVIES.
WELL, THEN, YOU'D BE MARRYING INTO ROYALTY.
なになにー?
WHAT I HEARD IS THAT NEGI-SENSEI IS, IN FACT, A PRINCE FROM A SMALL COUNTRY WHO'S HIDING HIS IDENTITY.
OH!
ワイ♡
CHATTER

IF I GET NEGI-SENSEI, I'LL BE A PRINCESS.

I HEARD NEGI-SENSEI'S WEIRDED OUT.

IT LOOKS LIKE PRINCE-NEGI LIKES PARTNERS.

WOW! THAT'S JUST LIKE A PRINCE.

NEGI-KUN IS LOOKING FOR A PARTNER AT A BALL.

THREE FASTEST MEANS OF SPREADING INFORMATION: TELEPHONE, TELEGRAPH, TELL A GIRL. WITHIN FIFTEEN MINUTES...

HO! IT WAS GETTING DANGEROUS BACK THERE.

IF IT GETS OUT I'M A WIZARD, I'D BE SENT BACK TO SCHOOL, AND MY GRANDFATHER SWORE HE'D TURN ME INTO A WEASEL IF THAT HAPPENED.

オコジョ ermine

I GOTTA BE CAREFUL NOT TO LET MY SECRET OUT.

THIS WHOLE PARTNER THING IS A DISTRACTION. BEST TO FORGET ABOUT IT.

FIRST I GOTTA CONCENTRATE ON SCHOOL TOMORROW.

I'M BEGGING YOU, PICK ME FOR A PARTNER!!
TROMP TROMP TROMP
ME TOO, ME TOO, PRINCE-NEGI!
WHOAH!!
YOU SAID YOU'RE LOOKING FOR A PARTNER!?
A LOVER! FIANCEE! BRIDE!?
WELL? WHEN'S THE ROYAL BALL!?
CHATTER
HOW SHOULD I KNOW!?
CHATTER
SENSEI, IS IT TRUE YOU'RE A PRINCE?
THAT STAFF IS LIKE AN IMPERIAL SCEPTER, ISN'T IT!
MAKE ME YOUR QUEEN!
WHAT'S EVERY-BODY TALKING ABOUT!?
RUNAWAY PRINCE! AFTER HIM!
DASH
WHAH!! THIS IS BAD!
TROMP TROMP
PRINCE-NEGI!
HUH?
WHOOSH

HE'S NOT HERE.
WHERE DID HE GO?
LET'S FIND HIM.
WHOA!! WHAT AM I GONNA DO? THE STORY'S TAKEN ON A LIFE OF ITS OWN!
I NEED A HIDEOUT FOR A WHILE!
THE SCHOOL SHOULD STILL BE EMPTY, AT LEAST UNTIL TOMORROW.
SHOO
WHEW. LOOKS LIKE I'M OK HERE.
HUH!?

YOU STARTLED ME.
UM...
HUH...
NOW I'VE DONE IT.
I'VE SHOWN MY MAGIC TO A COMPLETE STRANGER!?
WHOEVER YOU ARE, YOU SHOULD KNOW THERE'S, UHM... A CIRCUS. IN TOWN. AND WHAT YOU JUST SAW...
NEGI-KUN. NEGI-KUN!
IT'S A TRICK. WIRE WORK. I'M AN ACROBAT, YOU SEE, AND...
NEGI-KUN, IT'S ME!
HUH? ME...?
UH...
KO-
KONOKA-SAN!!
WHAT'S GOING ON? YOU CAME OUTTA NOWHERE AND SURPRISED ME.
ACROBAT? SH'RIGHT!

SO YOU DIDN'T SEE... I MEAN, GREAT! OKAY!

UH... BEAUTIFUL KIMONO YOU HAVE THERE.

THANKS. SO WHY ARE YOU HERE, NEGI-KUN?

KONOKA-SAMA!?

WHERE ARE YOU!?

IS THAT WHO I THINK IT...

YEAH. 'FRAID SO.

NEGI-KUN, I'VE GOTTA RUN!

ACTUALLY, SO DO I!

WHAT !?

YOU'RE ON AN O-MIAI !?

YUP. IT'S KIND OF MY GRANDFATHER'S HOBBY: SETTING UP O-MIAIS.
HE'S ALWAYS FORCING HIS RECOMMENDATIONS ON ME. SINCE IT'S JUST THE TWO OF US, HE'S DETERMINED TO FIND ME A FIANCÉ.

TODAY I HAD TO GO HAVE MY PICTURE TAKEN TO USE FOR AN O-MIAI.
I ESCAPED IN THE MIDDLE OF IT.
WOW! AN O-MIAI. AMAZING. ONE QUESTION:

WHAT'S AN O-MIAI?
HEH! YOU'RE TOO MUCH!
STOOP

AN O-MIAI IS A MARRIAGE PARTNER. BASICALLY, YOU GO OUT ON ARRANGED BLIND DATES IN HOPES OF FINDING YOUR FUTURE PARTNER.
UH... PARTNER?

RUSTLE
LOOK, THESE ARE ALL THE PHOTOS FROM POTENTIAL MATES.
WOW! THERE'S A LOT!

EVERYONE LOOKS PRETTY HANDSOME! THERE'S DOCTORS AND LAWYERS.
UH, WHOA! THIS GUY'S TWICE MY AGE.

I'M STILL A KID...
WHY SHOULD I HAVE TO DECIDE ON A HUSBAND?
YOU SHOULDN'T! I TOTALLY GET WHAT YOU'RE SAYING, KONOKA-SAN.
SPEAKING OF THAT, AREN'T YOU ALSO IN THE MIDDLE OF LOOKING FOR A PARTNER?
IF THAT'S SO, THEN— MORE THAN ANY OF THE GUYS MY GRAND-FATHER CHOSE—
I'D PREFER YOU AS MY PARTNER.
HUH?
YOU KNOW WHAT? I'LL HELP YOU DETERMINE YOUR IDEAL PARTNER.
HOW WILL YOU DO THAT?
LUCKY FOR YOU, I'M THE PRESIDENT OF THE FORTUNE TELLING CLUB.
YUP. MY LUCKY DAY, ALL RIGHT.
SPARKLE
I CAN TELL THAT YOU'LL BE A HANDSOME MAN...
NEGI AT 18.
SOME SAY FOREIGNERS MAKE THE BEST PARTNERS.
SHRIEK
IS THAT ME!?

CLASP

HMMM. UH HUH. INDEED.

H-HOW IS IT?

IT SEEMS LIKE KONOKA'S FORTUNE TELLING IS RIGHT ON TARGET.

NEGI-KUN'S FUTURE PARTNER IS...

IS EXTREMELY CLOSE.

HUH.

THAT'S OBVIOUSLY ASUNA-SAN!
YOU'RE NOT PREDICTING! YOU'RE JUST MAKING THAT UP!
PRETTY MUCH, YEAH.
BUT YOU LIKE ASUNA, RIGHT, NEGI-KUN?
WHA....LI...I DON'T LI-LIKE HER! NOT IN PARTICULAR.
FLUSTER
ドドド
AH HA HA! NEGI-KUN, YOU'RE FACE IS BEET RED.
ADMIT IT: YOU AND SHE HAVE BEEN GETTING ON WELL LATELY.
TH-THAT'S NOT TRUE.
じたばた
SQUIRM
ISN'T IT? IT'S DOING ASUNA SOME GOOD.
SHE SEEMS SO HAPPY LATELY.
ALSO, NEGI-KUN, I, TOO...
HUH?
SINCE YOU'VE COME, NEGI-KUN...
SQUEEZE
I'M HAPPY BECAUSE I'VE GOT A CUTE LITTLE BROTHER.

......
KONOKA-SAN...
I-I'M NOT A LITTLE BROTHER, I'M A TEACHER!
POW
NEGI-KUN'S ANGRY AGAIN.
SNAG
OH!
AAH!
WAAH!
THUD
HEH HEH
WHOA!
AH!
TEE HEE
NOW MY PANTIES HAVE BEEN SEEN.
UH, NO...
YOU TWO SEEM TO BE GETTING ON WELL.
WHAT!?

SHOCK
NEGI, WE WERE WORRIED AND CAME LOOKING FOR YOU.
KONOKA-SAN! ACTING SO MATURE, BUT TRYING TO SEDUCE NEGI-SENSEI AT THE FIRST OPPORTUNITY!
NO! THAT'S NOT IT AT ALL, CLASS REP-SAN.
SUNA, T'S ALL A ISTAKE.
A-ASUNA-SAN.
RUMBLE
HE'S OVER HERE!
POW
PRINCE-NEGI!
WHOA!
WE FOUND HIM!
MISS KONOKA!
ACK!
PRINCE-NEGI, PICK ME, PICK ME.
M-ME TOO.
MISS KONOKA, DON'T RUN AWAY TODAY.
MARRY INTO ROYALTY!
KONOKA-SAN, BEGGING OUT WON'T BE TOLERATED.
HELP ME ASUNA!
SUNA!
TO BE CONTINUED IN VOLUME 3

– STAFF –

Ken Akamatsu

Takashi Takemoto

Kenichi Nakamura

Masaki Ohyama

Keiichi Yamashita

Chigusa Amagasaki

Takaaki Miyahara

Kei Nishikawa

Thanks To

Ran Ayanaga

Toshiko Akamatsu

About the Creator

Negima! is only Ken Akamatsu's third manga, although he started working in the field in 1994 with *AI Ga Tomaranai*. Like all of Akamatsu's work to date, it was published in Kodansha's *Shonen Magazine*. *AI Ga Tomaranai* ran for five years before concluding in 1999. In 1998, however, Akamatsu began the work that would make him one of the most popular manga artists in Japan: *Love Hina*. *Love Hina* ran for four years, and before its conclusion in 2002, it would cause Akamatsu to be granted the prestigious Manga of the Year award from Kodansha, as well as going on to become one of the best-selling manga in the United States.

COMPILATION OF MATERIAL FOR THE BEGINNING SETTINGS OF NEGIMA!

THE ORIGINAL CHARACTER SKETCHES

THERE ARE MANY CHARACTERS THAT APPEAR IN NEGIMA! SO THREE ASSISTANTS AND I LIVE TOGETHER. WE DIVIDE THE WORK AND DECIDE THE MINUTE DETAILS OF THE SETTINGS. BECAUSE OF THIS, EVERY CHARACTER'S 'GROWING PAINS' ARE DIFFERENT. THIS TIME, WE'LL INTRODUCE THOSE SKETCH IDEAS.

—AKAMATSU.

MAGISTER NEGI MAGI

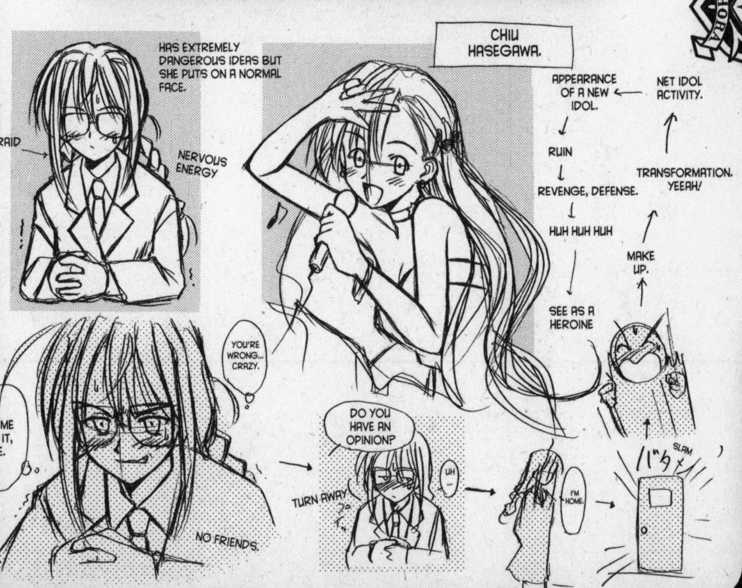

THE STORY PLAN FOR CHISAME IS NOT WRITTEN (HA HA). WE'RE MAKING IT UP AS WE GO. AT THE BEGINNING, THE TWINS DIDN'T HAVE MUCH PERSONALITY. IN THE FINAL VERSION THEY'RE A COUPLE OF PRANKSTERS. BUT THIS IS ALSO INTERESTING.

MAGISTER NEGI MAGI

I'M NOT SURE WHAT TO DO ABOUT THEIR NAMES. THEY'RE TWO PEOPLE WHO DON'T THINK ALIKE ABOUT ANYTHING. OCCASIONALLY, THEY CHUCKLE AND LAUGH TOGETHER.

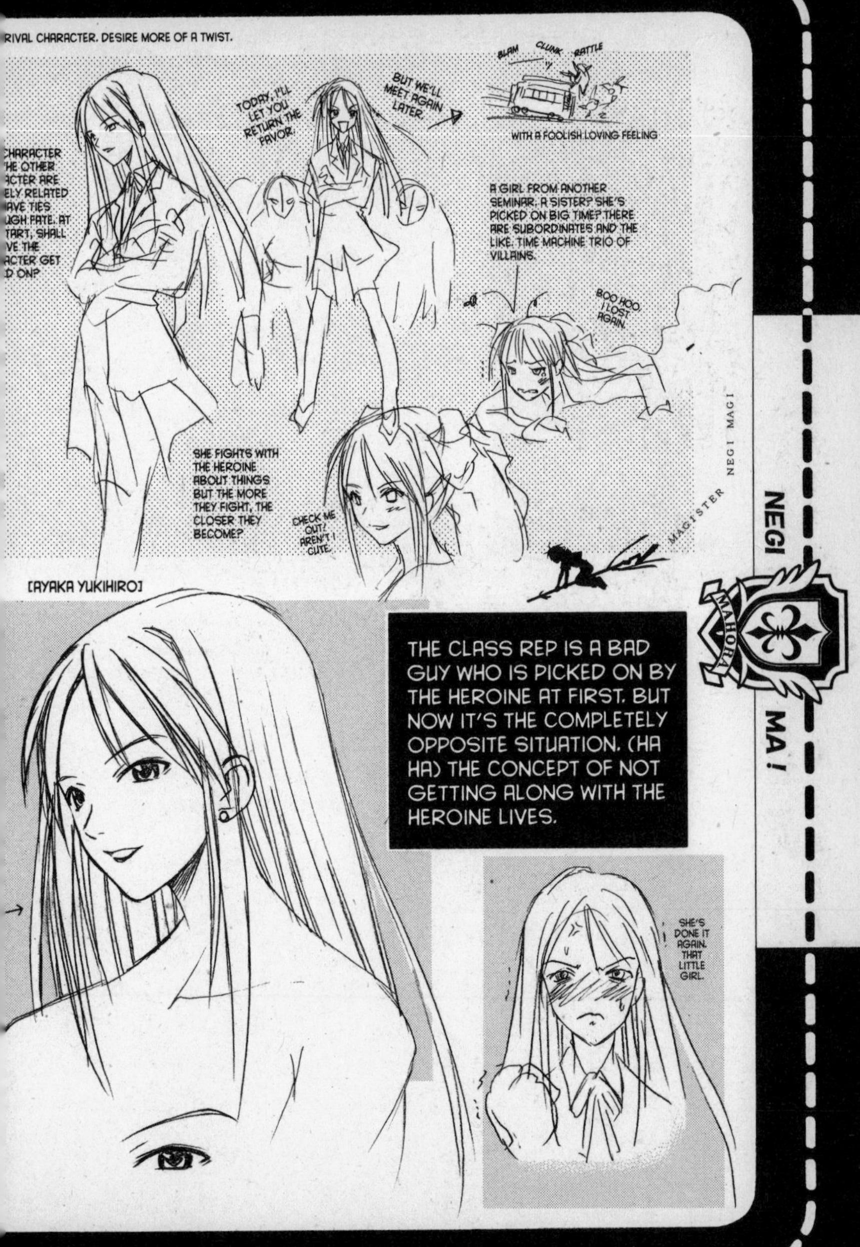
RIVAL CHARACTER. DESIRE MORE OF A TWIST.
CHARACTER
HE OTHER
ACTER ARE
ELY RELATED
HAVE TIES
UGH FATE. AT
TART, SHALL
VE THE
ACTER GET
D ON?
TODAY, I'LL LET YOU RETURN THE FAVOR.
BUT WE'LL MEET AGAIN LATER.
BLAM CLUNK RATTLE
WITH A FOOLISH LOVING FEELING
A GIRL FROM ANOTHER SEMINAR. A SISTER? SHE'S PICKED ON BIG TIME? THERE ARE SUBORDINATES AND THE LIKE. TIME MACHINE TRIO OF VILLAINS.
BOO HOO. I LOST AGAIN.
SHE FIGHTS WITH THE HEROINE ABOUT THINGS BUT THE MORE THEY FIGHT, THE CLOSER THEY BECOME?
CHECK ME OUT! AREN'T I CUTE.
[AYAKA YUKIHIRO]
MAGISTER NEGI MAGI
NEGI MA!
MAHORA
THE CLASS REP IS A BAD GUY WHO IS PICKED ON BY THE HEROINE AT FIRST. BUT NOW IT'S THE COMPLETELY OPPOSITE SITUATION. (HA HA) THE CONCEPT OF NOT GETTING ALONG WITH THE HEROINE LIVES.
SHE'S DONE IT AGAIN. THAT LITTLE GIRL.

MAGISTER NEGI MAGI

[KOZUE MIGARA]

A GENERAL PERSON. THE HEROINES CLOSE FRIEND WHO PLAY A FORCEFUL ROLE.

THIS IS CHARACTER DESIGNED AS THE ORIGINAL "HEROINE'S PAL". IT BECAME THE ORIGINAL PLAN FOR "MAKIE". SAKURAKO SPRANG FROM THE LACROSSE CLUB. HER POPULARITY WITH THE STAFF IS HIGH.

BY THE WAY, THE SERIAL NEGIMA! IN THE CHUKAN SHOUNEN MAGAZINE OFTEN HAS A CHARACTER POPULARITY VOTE. DEPENDING ON THIS, THEIR APPEARANCE FLUCTUATES SO EVERYONE PLEASE PARTICIPATE!

A GENERAL STUDENT. A GOOD FRIEND OF THE HEROINE. SEVERAL STRANGE INCIDENTS THAT THEY'RE THRUST INTO (IN THEIR HEARTS) APPEAR IN THE THIRD STORY. YOU CAN FEEL THE FATIGUE OF BEING INVOLVED. WHY THE SCHOOL IS THIS STRANGE IS IN QUESTION. INCREASINGLY, IT BECOMES AN ISSUE THAT MUST BE DEALT WITH.

LACROSSE CLUB

AN EXTREMELY NORMAL, REALISTIC PERSON WITH REGARDS TO BEING AWARE OF LOVE ETC.

LIBRARY DIRECTOR, SECOND YEAR HIGH SCHOOL.
I HAVE AN IMPRESSION OF THE LIBRARY (FAMILIAR RESEARCH ROOM) WHERE THE CHARACTER'S HANG OUT. THIS ROLE.
SMILE
SMILE
AH HA HA
あはは
ALWAYS LOOKING AT THE COUNTER.
LIKE A CAFÉ MASTER.
HMMMM
FLIP
I'D LIKE TO SEE MY FATHER'S RESEARCH DOCU-MENTS PLEASE.
GOOD AT COMPUTERS
THEY SEEM LIKE NICE PEOPLE
COUNTER
OK OK. I GOT IT.
THERE'S VALUE IN THESE SKETCHES (SOME PARTS ILLEGIBLE)
HELMET HEAD
NEGI
MAHORA
MA!
[MIEKO MIYAZAKI]
STYLE IS NOT GOOD.
BOOKSTORES DON'T REALLY CHANGE, DO THEY? AT PRESENT, I CAN'T BELIEVE THEY'RE THIS ACTIVE. ALL THE CHARACTERS' NAMES ARE STILL SUBJECT TO CHANGE. MIEKO IS STILL A WORK IN PROGRESS.
MAGISTER NEGI MAGI
WELL THEN, LET'S MEET AGAIN IN VOLUME 3! –♪

IDEAS FOR NEGIMA'S UNIFORMS.

MAGISTER NEGI MAGI

MAGISTER NEGI MAGI

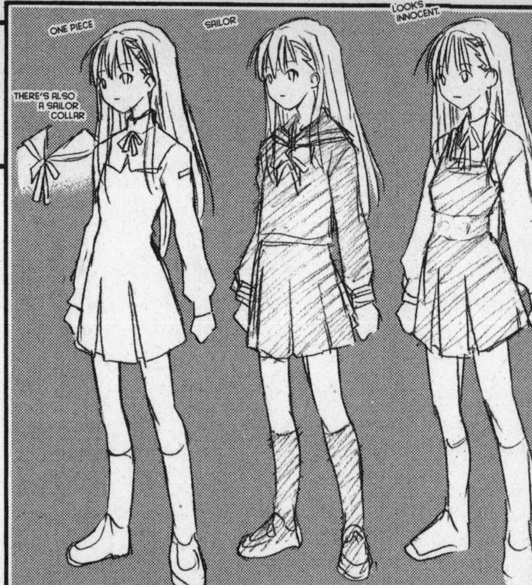

BECAUSE MAHORA ACADEMY ENCOMPASSES MANY SCHOOLS INCLUDING ELEMENTARY, JUNIOR HIGH, HIGH SCHOOL AND COLLEGE DIVISIONS (WITH ITS MANY RESPECTIVE SCHOOLS), THERE ARE MANY UNIFORMS. THE UNIFORM IDEAS INTRODUCED HERE ARE THE BASIC ONES FOR ASUNA AND THE LIKE FROM THE JUNIOR HIGH DEPARTMENT. EVENTUALLY, BY MAJORITY DECISION WE USED THE BLAZER WITH CHECK PATTERNED SKIRT. CONCERNING THE SCHOOL BADGE DESIGN, THERE ARE VARIOUS DESIGNS AND WE'LL GET TO THAT AT THE NEXT OPPORTUNITY (HA HA)!
COMPILED BY ASHI MAX.

LATIUM LEXICON NEGIMARIUM

Compiled by Minoru Ashi

Magister Negi Magi. Magic-Sensei Negima is the subtitle in the Japanese edition. Well, Latin is used everywhere in the world. Here, *magister* means *sensei*. *Negi* is a proper name. *Magi* means *magical*. Basically, it translates to Wizard Negi-Sensei. (So what in the world does the 'ma' in *Negima!* mean?)

The Latin used in *Negima!* has cases where the long vowels are not extended owing to the convenience of rhythm. For example, *magi* is actually pronounced *ma-gee* but as he is often called *ma-jai* so he comes to be called *magi*.

Magister Magi also means magical people. Magi is the plural case of *wizard*. The singular nominative case is *magus*. Magister here means *people*. As written above, it also means *sensei* and is equivalent to the English *master* and the German *meister*.

Melchizedek. The Vulgata translation of the Bible (Genesis 14:17-20) says that upon returning from the subjugation of Cherdorlaomer and the kings who were allied with him, King Sodom came to meet Abram in Valley Shaveh. The king of Salem, Melchizedek, a priest of the supreme god, came there bringing bread and wine. Melchizedek said blessings to Abram. The blessing asked of the supreme god, creator of heaven and earth, was for Abram. The blessing also promised to deliver the enemy into the clutches of the supreme god. In Hebrew, it's Melchizedek. It's not written in the canons or Apocrypha, but there's a legend of our ancestor Abraham being granted the secret of cabala. (Eighth Period.)

Minister magi means a 'follower of magic' and is equivalent to the English term *minister*. In the case of women, they are called *ministra magi*. The relationship between the magi as an individual and as a master of magic has many factors, and the role the minister plays varies in response to that. Today, there are a lot of partners who become lovers and spouses, but partners aren't always limited to the opposite sex. For more on this, refer to Negima Volume 3.

- **Rastel maskil magister.** This is not Latin (and that language is the key to releasing magic), and it seems like it's a code with no meaning. *Rastel maskil magister* is the exclusive incantation for Negi Springfield. Each and every wizard thinks of one for themselves, and Negi came up with his own when he graduated from magic school. In the case of simple magic, you can abbreviate it. (First used in Second Period.)

- **Age nascatur, potio amoris.** Literally: well, in life, a love potion. This is a spell for th preparation of magic medicine. *Potio* means potion in Latin. Used for the purification love potions. (Second Period.)

- **Aer aer amplificet mammas.** Air, atmosphere, breasts expand. Negi calls on the power of a friendly air spirit to manipulate the air. In this case, it created an air bubble around Asuna's chest, making it seem like she had huge breasts. To actually change Asuna's appearance, Negi would have needed to use the spell *mammae crescant*, which means, in short, "breasts become larger!" (Third Period.)

- **Salent, penicili.** Dance, brushes. Making things move is basic magic. (Fourth Period.)

- **Aer...** Magic word meaning air. Used by Negi, angry at the attack by Black Lily from the dodge ball club, to call on the air spirit. In the previous panel, an air current was starting to happen. However, in the middle of the incantation he was hit by Asuna, so just how powerful the spell is remains a mystery. (Sixth Period.)

- **Tria fila nigra prommissiva, mihi limitationem per tres dies.** Three black pledge strings, a restriction on myself for three days. A spell that Negi cast on himself, bottling up his own magic power. Can also be used to contain the magic of enemies who posses magic powers. (Seventh Period.)

- **Undecim spiritus lucis, coeuntes segittant inimicum, sagitta magica.** The 11 pillars of spirit light! Come gather and light up my enemy, magic archer. *Sagitta magic* means magic arrow. *Spiritus* is 'spirit' in English. Calling on a minor spirit, it's a spell that shoots the enemy you're facing. Depending on the spirit you call on, the effect is different. A rudimentary battle spell, but the scope of its application is wide. (Tenth Period.)

- **Fragrantia floris, amicis vigorem, vitalitatem, auram salutarem refectio.** The fragrance of a flower, a wind that will fill my friends with energy, vitality, and health. Complete energy recovery. The flower that Negi uses is the catalyst. That catalyst makes it easier to cast the spell and heightens the effect. A spell that refreshes one's mood.

1. SAYO AIZAKA

1940~

DON'T CHANGE HER SEATING

2. YUNA AKASHI

BASKETBALL TEAM

PROFESSOR AKASHI'S DAUGHTER

3. KAZUMI ASAKU

SCHOOL NEWSPAPER

MAHORA NEWS (ext. 809-

4. YUE AYASE

KID'S LIT CLUB
PHILOSOPHY CLUB
LIBRARY CLUB

5. AKO IZUMI

NURSE'S OFFICE
SOCCER TEAM
(NON-SCHOOL ACTIVITY)

6. AKIRA OKOCHI

SWIM TEAM

7. KAKIZAKI MISA

CHEERLEADER
CHORUS

A GOOD PERSON JUST AS I THOUGHT.

8. ASUNA KAGURAZAKA

ART CLUB

HAS A TERRIBLE KICK.

9. KASUGA MISORA

10. CHACHAMARU RAKUSO

TEA CEREMONY CLUB
GO CLUB

CALL ENGINEERING (ext. A08-7796) IN CASE OF EMERGENCY

MADOKA

11. MADOKA KUGIMIYA

CHEERLEADER

FEI KU

12. FEI KU

CHINESE MARTIAL ARTS
GROUP

RANDAUGHTER OF SCHOOL DEAN

KONOKA KONOE

SECRETARY
RTUNE-TELLING CLUB
LIBRARY CLUB

HARUNA SAOTOME

MANGA CLUB
LIBRARY CLUB

SETSUNA SAKURAZAKI

TSUNA SAKURAZAKI

JAPANESE FENCING

YOTO SHINMEI STYLE

MAKIE SASAKI

GYMNASTICS

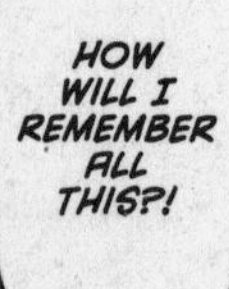

20. KAEDE NAGASE
WALKING CLUB
VERY DETERMINED

May God speed you, Negi.
Takamichi T. Takahata

ranslation Notes

panese is a tricky language for most westerners, and translation is often
ore art than science. For your edification and reading pleasure, here are
otes on some of the places where we could have gone in a different
irection in our translation of the work, or where a Japanese cultural
ference is used.

alf and Half, page 6

n this context in Japanese, the term "half" used here indicates mixed
ncestry, so we gave it the closest English translation: "half-breed."

aseball Janken, page 11

anken is the Japanese name for "rock, paper, scissors," but this version is
sually played as a drinking game accompanied by a song about baseball that
ncorporates the "safe" and "out" rules used in baseball. If one loses, or gets
ut, you have to remove articles of clothing so it's something like strip
nken.

Mattcha Cola, page 19

Mattcha is a high-grade green tea used in the traditional Japanese Tea Ceremony.

Safe! page 25

The word being used to describe the library in Japanese is *matomo*, which means honest, decent or proper, not safe. But because Japanese is such a contextual language, it's meant to indicate that the library is free of traps, or safe.

Kotatsu, page 29

A *kotatsu* is a low table with a blanket placed under it that covers the legs. A small heater is underneath the table keeping your feet warm. Older *kotatsus* have a sunken floor where you can stretch your legs.

Sessha, page 71

Sessha is a condescending word that samurais used to refer to themselves. It also refers to a character from a book written in the 17th century that assisted women down on their luck.

Make Cake, Not Love, page 128

The literal translation of what Negi's sister said to him was "Love cake rather than love make," which means eating (or surviving) is more important than other things like love. In this context, however, it means "you can't judge a book by its cover."

Dango, page 133

Actually, what this said in Japanese was "More like a dango than a flower." A *dango* is a roasted rice ball that comes on a stick, usually three at a time.

Ojou-sama, page 138

Ojou-sama is a way of referring to the daughter or sister of someone with high political or social status.

O-miai, page 166

An *O-miai* is a date set up usually by one's parents, where information about each person is exchanged. Kind of like a blind date. Ideally, it leads to marriage. *O-miai* are becoming less popular in Japan as people seek to find their own partners. However, they are still used for people who for some reason or another have trouble finding a mate.

Preview of Volume Three

Here is an excerpt from Volume 3, on sale in English now.

か風強いですねー…！
サァァ…
ちょっと急ごうかなー
CANS SHOP
POCARI SWEAT
UCC

こ…こわくない～～～♪
…こわくないです～
こわくないかも～～♪

ざわっ…
こわっ…
びくっ

……？

ザザァァッ
え…

トッ！
ひ……

27番宮崎のどかか・・・・
テッ・・・
悪いけど少しだけその血を分けてもらうよ
キャアアアアアアッ!
バッ
ザアッ!!
待てーっ
!!
ぼ・・・
ラス・テル マ・スキル・・・
僕の生徒に何をするんですかーっ
風の精霊11人 縛鎖となりて 敵を捕まえろ
うーん・・・
ふらっ

サギタ・マギカ アエール・カプトゥーラエ
魔法の射手・戒めの風矢!!
もう気付いたか
氷楯・・・・
レフレクシオー
やっぱ気になるから本屋ちゃん送ってくよ
あ アスナーー
バキキキキ
!!
僕の呪文を全部はね返した!?
ややっぱり犯人は・・・・

ゴォオォオォ…
魔法使い……!?
くっ…
驚いたぞ
凄まじい
魔力だな……

えっ……
き 君は
ウチのクラスの…
エ…エヴァン
ジェリンさん!?

フフ……
新学期に入ったことだし
改めて歓迎のご挨拶と
行こうか 先生
…いや ネギ・
スプリングフィールド

10歳にして
この力……
さすがに
奴の息子だけは
ある

Also Available from Del Rey *Imagine*™

HAVE SPACE SUIT—WILL TRAVEL
by Robert A. Heinlein
Kip was willing to give up a lot to get to the moon—
but he never expected it to be his life!
On sale now

SWORD OF SHANNARA Parts 1-3
by Terry Brooks
"If Harry Potter has given you a thirst for fantasy and
you have not discovered the magic of Terry Brooks,
you are in for a treat."
—*Rocky Mountain News*
On sale now

DRAGONFLIGHT by Anne McCaffrey
The thrilling adventure of a girl, a dragon,
and the special bond they share. . . .
On sale now

ORPHAN STAR by Alan Dean Foster
One man in the Universe holds the key
to the mystery of Flinx's past—
and that man is trying to kill him!
On sale now

TUNNEL IN THE SKY by Robert A. Heinlein
For Rod Walker and his high school classmates, a simple
test has turned into a life-or-death nightmare.
On sale now

Published by Del Rey
Available wherever books are sold

TOMARE!

[STOP!]

You're going the wrong way!

Manga is a completely different type of reading experience.

To start at the *beginning*, go to the *end*!

That's right! Authentic manga is read the traditional Japanese way—from right to left. Exactly the *opposite* of how American books are read. It's easy to follow: Just go to the other end of the book, and read each page—and each panel—from right side to left side, starting at the top right. Now you're experiencing manga as it was meant to be.